A BITTER HEART

Peter Farquhar

'My fancy: I might hear his cry:
A bitter heart that bides its time and bites'

(Robert Browning: 'Caliban upon Setebos')

AuthorHouse™ UK Ltd.
500 Avebury Boulevard
Central Milton Keynes, MK9 2BE
www.authorhouse.co.uk
Phone: 08001974150

© 2012 Peter Farquhar. All rights reserved.

No part of this book may be reproduced, stored in a retrieval system, or transmitted by any means without the written permission of the author.

Published by AuthorHouse 9/17/2012

ISBN: 978-1-4772-2345-1 (sc)
ISBN: 978-1-4772-2600-1 (e)

This book is printed on acid-free paper.

The views expressed in this work are solely those of the author and do not necessarily reflect the views of the publisher, and the publisher hereby disclaims any responsibility for them.

This book is dedicated to STEVEN THOMPSON, whose advice, encouragement and suggestions were invaluable.

Special thanks must also go to TOBY MARSHALL for the cover design and to BEN FIELD for proof reading and necessary emendations.

'A BITTER HEART' can be read and appreciated even by Arsenal supporters.'

(Karin Eyles)

'I always wait for the 45. It goes to Cheadle Hulme, where respectable folks live.'
(the late Henry Farrington)

ONE

SHE WAS INSTANTLY AWARE OF the water's overpowering, icy energy. The river was the colour of unsettled ale; it was flowing fast, swollen by the recent heavy late October rain. The shock of colliding with this unfamiliar, hostile medium rapidly gave way to the panic of absolute terror. She could not swim. The current swept her along. It was not just that she was sinking. It was as though some malignantly destructive force of immense power was violently pulling her under. She screamed, horribly aware of her impending doom, but the sound seemed to tinkle hopelessly in space, her head bobbing above the immense, empty surface of the river as it drove relentlessly and dispassionately onwards.

He ran along the tow-path to keep up with her, struggling to divest his garments as he went. Stripped to his t-shirt and boxers, he leapt into the water. But the river seemed to acknowledge him with equal disregard. He did not reach her. He was aware of a shout from the bank towards which he was carried by a subordinate current. A pair of strong arms pulled him upwards through mud and reeds.

A young woman's body was washed up further downstream. The police were able to establish identification from the little purse zipped inside her heavy, water-logged fleece.

∼

Now, he sat with her widowed mother. The tea in the wide-rimmed Spode cup had become cold. His plate for the chocolate sponge cake was empty save for a few discarded crumbs.

'I know I keep saying it, Mrs Braithwaite………..'

'Oh, please, Rob — do call me Mara,'

'Er, well, um, Mara, er, I know I keep saying it, but I'm just so sorry. I was so utterly useless.'

'No! No! Rob, you did everything you could. You know I think that. You risked your own life. The policeman said that you were heroic. They don't say that unless they mean it. You mustn't keep on blaming yourself like this. Another cup of tea?'

'No thanks. I just keep going over it and rehearsing the same old thing.'

'Another slice of chocolate sponge cake?'

He demurred with a gesture of his hand.

'You know, I can't get the image of those last moments I saw her out of my mind. Oh, God! I'm so sorry.'

His eyes again filled with tears. He blew his nose into a soiled handkerchief.

The raw emotion was infectious. Mara Braithwaite started to weep gently herself. They were partners in grieving: the widowed mother having lost her only daughter and the daughter's young boyfriend's second devastating encounter with tragedy.

'Accidents are so dramatic, so violent.' Mara struggled to articulate the words.

'Yeah. It's the sort of thing that happens in the news — to other people. God — what a cliché!'

Mara Braithwaite looked at Rob. What a handsome boy he is, she thought, with his dark hair and eyes and his finely sculpted cheek-bones, his jaw defined by unshaven fleece. What a good-looking couple they would have made. He would be a good swimmer with his lean, athletic frame. The river must just have been too strong.

She herself looked less than her fifty years, with her neat blond hair, cut short, her hazel eyes, her curving bosom and hips separated by a slim waist. She wore a crisp white blouse and a sensible, well pressed skirt. She had lost interest in clothes since her husband's death.

'And it's not the first tragic death you've had in your twenty years of life, Rob.'

'My Mum,' he said simply, looking down at the carpet.

'If ever you want to talk about it — you know you can — with me, I mean.'

'Thanks. That's kind. Dad shuts up like a clam the moment it might be mentioned.'

'It must have been awful for him too.'

'The cancer was so quick. We'd been on holiday in France; she was fine- and then she was dead six weeks later.'

'Oh, Rob!' She wanted to get up and hug him but held back. 'And you've got no brothers and sisters to share your grief with. And now I'm on my own. I was an only child too. And now I've lost both my husband and my own only child.' Her eyes moistened but she retained her dignity. 'It's probably quite the wrong thing to suggest but- I hesitate to say it- perhaps I could share you with your father? Treat you as my son?'

'And you could be my surrogate mother?'

She wasn't sure whether he was extending an invitation or questioning the idea, possibly even with disfavour. She dare not press it.

But, when he rose to go, he put his arms round her in embrace. He was clean and fresh and firm, light but strong; his body was faintly scented with a subtly dry deodorant. She was sorry to see him leave.

TWO

THREE MONTHS EARLIER, KATE HAD been helping her mother to prepare lunch for a visit to be made by her uncle and aunt. It was a hot Saturday in August in the middle of the university vacation. Kate was feeling a little sorry for her mother as Mara was struggling through the first summer after her bereavement. At the same time, she was somewhat bored and the prospect of sitting through lunch with a brave, quietly grieving mother and her well meaning but somewhat sanctimonious aunt and uncle (her late father's brother) did not seem a good way of spending a Saturday in high summer. Still, there were compensations. She appreciated her mother's culinary skills and the prospect of *saumon-en-croute* was appealing. In any case, she had arranged to go clubbing in central Manchester with old school friends in the evening.

She was spending some nights at home during the long summer vacation, but was gradually easing herself into the first floor flat in Didsbury which Rob and she would be sharing with two other students. When applying to read Psychology two years ago, Kate had decided to go to Manchester University, rather than further afield, so that she could still have ready access to various friends, many of whom had attended the same independent girls' school in south Manchester. She did want to secure some measure of independence from home and so a stage of compromise had been reached. Having spent the first year in a hall of residence, she was now really looking forward to sharing the flat. It was quite spacious, situated in a large Edwardian red-brick villa in one of those tree-lined suburban residential streets running between the two arteries of Wilmslow Road and Kingsway. The number 45 bus ran past regularly on the main road to take Kate either south to her mother in Cheadle Hulme or north to the university and the centre of the city. Kate was to have a room at the front of the house and, at this time of the year, the broad leaves of an old plane tree almost touched the bow-window. Mara had found it a pleasant diversion to go bargain hunting with her daughter as they bought various drapes and covers and rugs and chatted about colour schemes.

'It's amazing what you can pick up at the Oxfam shop,' said Mara. 'This cover will transform the moth-eaten sofa and — look! It could have been made to match the curtains!'

Kate was grateful to her mother for her enthusiastic participation and her quick and practised eye. She guessed how sad her mother must be and that her deeper thoughts were bound to be retrospective, the best years of her life likely to have been in the past. Kate herself had flashes of nostalgia. Some of these were sufficiently powerful to produce a quick burst of tears. She remembered her father reading Enid Blyton to her in bed, helping her to make a sandcastle on the beach at Bispham, taking her by the hand to buy an ice-cream from the van which played the Teddy Bears' Picnic. Now, however, a young woman, and looking forward to her developing independence, as she chose to share this flat with the boy of her dreams, the bright sunlight outside, given voice by the call of some doves, beckoned her forwards into happiness. As posters were being stuck to the walls and cuddly toys put on the bed with its new bedspread, she caught her heart with a silent impulse of joy.

Mara was pleased to see her daughter happy. She loved Kate with the totality which only a mother could but she knew that the surest way to lose her would be to cling.

Now, however, lunch was ready and the visitors were arriving. A clean floral cloth had been placed over the garden table, neatly secured by cutlery and glasses. A clear rectangular vase containing pink roses was placed in the centre of the table. A large cream-coloured umbrella generously shaded the four chairs from the strong noon-tide sun. A blackbird, no longer serenading them as he had done as recently as two months earlier, took a bright-eyed interest in the possibility of sharing the feast as he hopped close to the border whence the roses had come.

Norman and Jane Kershaw arrived with a bunch of yellow scented lilies. They hugged and kissed mother and daughter in turn. Norman, Harry's brother, was a tall, gaunt Lancastrian with a pale face, spectacles and thinning grey hair. Jane was short and slightly plump with rosy cheeks and bright dark eyes which seemed to be perpetually smiling.

'Oh! Mara! Doesn't your table look really lovely!' she trilled, beaming with approval.

'Sorry we're a trifle late,' said Norman. He spoke with a modulated, educated voice, faintly inflected with the broad vowels of North Manchester. 'We'd have been here sooner but there was a heck of a jam on the M62 — at the Worsley junction with the M61. I don't know what had happened. There didn't seem to be any reason for it.'

'I think it was just every-one getting out and about on a sunny Saturday,' qualified his wife, ever keen to brighten any dark colour. 'It's not as if we get weather like this every week-end in Manchester!'

Kate involuntarily stopped listening. It wasn't as though she felt particularly hostile to her uncle and aunt; she just found them painfully dull, the more so as she grew older. She created in her mind's eye the image of Rob. They had been texting each other regularly but this morning he had called on her mobile. He was staying with two other lads in the *residence secondaire* of one of his old school friend's parents in the Lot valley. Apparently it was even hotter there. When they had spoken, he was lying beside a pool. She knew exactly what he would look like and dearly wished she could have been beside him. She visualised him in a pair of shorts, with his slim, supple six foot body draped on a sun bed. The handsome face would be decorated by a fast growing dark beard- not out of any consideration for fashion but because he had not bothered to shave. She imagined him rubbing sun cream onto his bare shoulders and then to his arms and legs and wished achingly that she was doing that for him. She had been thrilled by the sound of his deep, slightly husky, casual, modern public school voice, tinged with the usual humour.

'We went clubbing in Cahors last night. Not exactly the bright lights of dear old Manchester — but there were some nice Froggie chicks,' he had added with, she had to assume, unconscious tactlessness. He had laughed. Was he teasing her?

Normally, this was a trait she rather liked about Rob but, on this occasion, the remark left her feeling nettled, excluded and slightly anxious. Her mood had changed abruptly. No girl, she thought, could fail to find him attractive and she wondered just how far he might have taken things, especially after, no doubt, quite a few drinks. And he could speak French well- far better than she could. Several times in recent months, she had wondered to herself how Rob could ever have thought of returning the feelings which she had for him. He had been to boarding school and lived with his father in a terraced town-house in Chelsea. She had never been invited. He seemed too open and genuinely affectionate ever to be bothered about class but his constantly unruffled social confidence sometimes unnerved her. He moved through every situation with ease, flavoured with an amusement at life which she envied but could never emulate. Kate had rather liked her circumscribed, bourgeois, suburban life, centred around the impeccably tidy, spic-and-span semi-detached house in Cheadle Hulme, the social focus being school, reached by the same number 45 bus, just two miles further into the city than the flat which she was now organising. Now, she worried that the dashing Rob would suddenly, one black day, find her- blonde, petite, mousey, ordinary, conscious of speaking with a flat south Manchester accent- laughably provincial. She could not wait to share a flat with him — she almost caught her breath with the thrill of the anticipated daily intimacy —but, increasingly, she was frightened of the prospect too. Could she ever realistically hope to hold him, to keep him? Well, she was certainly going to do everything in her power to succeed.

Now, however, she was jerked out of her reverie by an uncomfortable pause following a question which her Auntie Jane had just put to her.

'So, Katie, how's this wonderful new flat which we've been hearing about? Tell your Uncle Norman and me about it.'

The enquiry was generous in spirit and the smile genuine. A year ago, Kate would have welcomed it warmly. Now, however, she found it irritating, patronising and intrusive. Her new world needed to be off limits to her uncle and auntie. She had recently become annoyed too that she still seemed to have to call them 'Uncle' and 'Auntie'. Rob would have long since 'cut the crap', to quote the man himself.

'It's nothing special,' she affected. 'Somewhere to live, not too far from the university itself.' Then, feigning moderate enthusiasm, 'No: it's OK!'

'Oh! Your Mummy said that it was really good and that you'd both been buying up the shops to make it extra nice,' encouraged Auntie Jane, smiling indulgently.

'Yes, Kate,' interjected Mara, slightly surprised by her daughter's reduction of the project which they had both endorsed so heartily, or so she had thought. 'You've been really keen about sorting it all out. What's this sudden indifference? '

Then, addressing her sister-in-law, 'Perhaps the heat's getting to her,' she said, smiling at her stony-faced offspring. 'We've had a great time fixing it all up: matching colours, choosing rugs, buying mugs and the basic cutlery and a kettle. You know the sort of thing; I've found it quite fun- and I thought, until this moment, so did Kate.'

'Yes — yes, I did, Mum. Thanks.'

There was an awkward pause.

Auntie Jane was more warm-hearted than tactful and managed to be supremely maladroit as she changed the subject.

'And I hear from your Mummy that you've got this smashing boy-friend. What's his name again?' She gave Kate a cheeky, knowing smile.

'Rob,' announced Kate without embellishment.

Mara rushed into the void.

'Oh, Jane — he's a really wonderful chap. It's truly lovely when he comes round. If I say so myself, my daughter couldn't have chosen better!' She beamed meaningfully at Kate.

Uncle Norman vaguely detected a scent of humour in the air and decided to invest it with a little Mancunian flavour.

'Is he right for use as well as ornament?' he chuckled.

Kate blushed in silent anger. The two ladies stalled.

'Oh dear,' he recanted. 'I can see that that could be taken more ways than one. I didn't mean anything nasty. You surely know that!'

'No, no! We mustn't tease Katie, Norman,' interposed his wife, who, noticing her niece's reaction, was sincerely concerned not to upset her.

Mara too moved quickly to defuse any mild discomfort.

'No, really, he is an exceptionally nice boy. He's always welcome here and I'm very happy for Kate. They'll get on really well together in the flat with the others. My only sorrow is that I imagine that I'll see less of them both but that's selfish and I'm not going to inflict self-pity on Kate.'

Uncle Norman, however, was not the quickest one to adapt tone.

'I understand that he's a Londoner. I hope, Katie, that you've told him the truth about Manchester. You know….'

'I suppose you mean, "What Manchester thinks today, London thinks tomorrow," replied Katie, striving for patience. 'Well, no, I haven't, because I don't think it's true.'

'No, no,' responded her uncle benignly. 'It might have been true in the Nineteenth Century when John Bright was giving his great speeches here, trying to persuade the Tory Government to relax restrictions on trade, but it's all much the same now, wherever you are. It's all decided by these bureaucrats in Brussels.'

'Oh, don't start on about that, Norman, please,' implored his wife, still smiling in good humour.

Kate felt less threatened as the conversation moved into less intimate territory. Uncle Norman was very knowledgeable about history, particularly local history, and, as a child, she had always rather liked and respected him. She had also appreciated her aunt's kindness over the years. But, Rob and the flat — these were to be held on a different plane of existence and had nothing to do with them. Her mother was different. Partly, she had to be accommodated in the scheme of things but also, she deserved to be. Kate had been relieved that Mara had taken so warmly to Rob and she loved Rob all the more for having been not just charming to her mother but gracious — yes, definitely gracious.

Jane changed the subject decisively.

'So- we've got to ask- how are you coping now, Mara?' she asked, leaning forward solicitously. 'We all miss dear Harry but it's worst of all for you. You know that Norman and I are always here for you- and for Katie too.'

'Oh well,' responded Mara, simultaneously upset by the introduction of the subject but grateful for the concern. 'You know —'. She broke off, unable to go any further.

'You'd be more than welcome to come up of a Sunday for lunch. Perhaps you'd like to go to church with us beforehand?'

'Thank you. You've mentioned this before. You know I don't believe in all that.'

'It might help you, you know.'

Mara felt forced to resist.

''If God existed and He loved some-one like me, He wouldn't have taken my dear Harry. You mustn't pester me with religion, Jane. It might work for you but it doesn't for me.' She had raised her voice and felt tears forming in her eyes.

Jane rose and went towards Mara but stopped, instinctively aware that it would be a mistake to hug her.

'Oh, I'm sorry. I didn't mean to hurt you, my love.'

'Easy now, Jane,' cautioned her husband. 'Easy does it; sit down.'

Kate willed the image of Rob beside the French swimming pool into the front of her imagination. How she wished she was by his side.

THREE

'Well, Mrs Braithwaite, that was a wonderful steak and kidney pie. Thank you.'

'Yes, Mum: you're a star — once again!'

'Not at all. It's just lovely to have you both.'

Mara was indeed extremely happy to see them. It was a miserably wet Sunday in late October and she had been feeling the great hurt of her loss. She had wept when visiting the cemetery in Cheadle yesterday. Her flimsy umbrella had been useless against the Manchester rain as it swept in horizontally from the west. No-one else was there: just the dead, and Harry, who was also dead, but yet different from all these other faceless ghosts, as he was distinctive, still somehow painfully half alive, still part of her.

Additionally, although Mara could not admit it to her daughter, she terribly missed having Kate around. She had accepted a part-time voluntary job with the Citizens'

Advice Bureau. It had taken her out of the house but her mind and her heart were elsewhere. But elsewhere was nowhere. It was in the past with her husband, or else in the impossible present with her daughter and Rob, who, she was starting to feel, really was like a son- except that, of course, he wasn't. Even now, when they were both here with her, she knew that, in an hour or so, they would be gone. They were decent young people but she recognised, possibly better than they did themselves, that they were here to humour her. She guessed that they probably felt sorry for her but in their hearts they were looking forward to the recaptured freedom of just being with each other again. She didn't resent this but it did nothing to alleviate her grieving isolation.

Mara had been attending computer classes. The computer had been very definitely in Harry's zone of control, a state of affairs which she had welcomed. Since his death, however, she had been struggling to learn how to master it. She needed to use it at the CAB but, there, she had learnt the necessary basic routines and, in any case, if she got stuck, there was always somebody else to help her, possibly even one of the clients themselves. When something went wrong at home, she was completely stuck. Still feeling cautious about spending money after her bereavement, she was not willing to pay for a computer technician to come out, blind her with technicalities and then charge the earth. She just waited for Kate, or possibly Norman, to help her when they next visited.

For the past few days, she had been unable to access her e-mail. She could see that there had been two messages from a cousin in Florida but she could not open them. After lunch, Kate and Rob had accompanied her to the little spare bedroom which she now regarded as her 'office'. Rob took charge and, in less than five minutes, had released the messages and had explained what she had done wrong. She actually understood what he was saying; he was so clear and patient and always wearing that smile of good will. She hoped with all her heart that all would be well with them both. She hoped they would stick together. Rob would be such a support for Kate and- yes, she might as well admit it- possibly for Mara herself in the future.

Kate and Rob came downstairs again, insisted on loading the dish-washer, had a cup of coffee and left.

～

They had now been in the flat for six weeks. There were four of them altogether. As well as Kate and Rob, there were Jess and Woody. Jess was a tall, shapely, dark-haired, sloe-eyed, languidly self-confident young woman. She was part of the ménage because, like Rob, she was taking a degree which included French and they had met the previous year at a weekly seminar. Jess had come from a girls' boarding school in the south of England. She was socially assured, like Rob, accustomed to living away from home among people of her own age. She was combining French with History of Art whereas Rob was combining it with English.

Woody (whose real name was Christopher Wood) was a scientist who spent the equivalent of office hours working in laboratories in a central site at the university. He had attended a Buckinghamshire grammar school. Small and hairy, with light brown hair and bright hazel-brown eyes, like Rob careless about shaving, slightly diffident, with a quietly self-deprecating sense of humour, he was popular with many of the girls who generally regarded him as 'sweet' or 'cute'. He too was there because of Rob. They had played football together in a low-key friendly team during their first term, a year ago. In what is arguably the capital city of soccer, they had occasionally teamed up with some other lads to make the pilgrimage to Old Trafford, where they could enjoy the spectacle of Ferguson's men dispatching visiting teams from all over the country. Rob liked Woody a lot, accepting warmly his unexpected sense of benignly cynical quiet humour. He regarded Woody as a decent bloke, a real mate, 'a regular guy'. Sharing with the two girls, there were moments when he enjoyed being lads together, comrades in arms against any perceived threat of domestic tyranny. Woody was very self-sufficient, as unfazed by the negotiation of daily routine domestically and academically as Rob and Jess. He was the best cook in the flat. His various pasta dishes were enjoyed by all, especially Rob.

Although it was so near home for her, geographically at least, Kate was the least equipped of the four to enter into the communal life required and she had rapidly realised that it would be considerably more difficult than she had idealised in her imagination during the warm empty days of the summer. She had been cherishing a montage of Rob and her, sharing little intimacies together, going shopping, sitting on a sofa with mugs of coffee as they watched T.V., his arm perhaps round her shoulder. Somehow or other, the other two had been distant shadows, floating about on the periphery of this ideal, helping to pay the rent.

But it was not working out like that at all. For a start, Rob knew the other two and she did not. She immediately felt socially intimidated by Jess and, although Woody was pleasant enough when she saw him, his association was obviously primarily with Rob and she felt excluded. There was a communal room which did indeed have a television, a sofa, two armchairs and a coffee table. The two lads would regularly monopolise it, put their feet up on the table, drink beer out of cans, watch football and drop empty crisp packets on the floor.

At such times, Jess might be out of the house with her own friends. When she was back, however, her relationship with Rob was one of easy familiarity. This surprised Kate and she resented it. But, after a fortnight or so, it was Jess who was keeping more to her room. This was because her new boy-friend, Eddie, a handsome rugby player from a North London comprehensive, was coming round regularly. Eddie, with his neatly compact muscular frame, his café latte skin and sporting a little moustache, was studying Sports Science and spoke not unlike Ali Gee. Kate thought that they seemed oddly matched. Once, when no-one else was around, she listened outside the door of Jess's room. Jess and Eddie had been in there a long time. Kate was not so naïve as to imagine that they had spent an hour or so just holding hands. Now she could hear them together: little deep groans of satisfaction from Eddie and high-pitched giggles from Jess, the occasional sound of heavy physical movement on the bed. She wondered just how undressed they were. Were they completely naked or were they in their underwear? Eddie would look good in his boxer shorts. As she heard the wordless sounds of what might be orgasmic climax, Kate indulged her imagination. Who, she wondered, was lying on top of whom? Or were they both lying on their sides? Whichever way it was, Jess would surely be wrapping her long legs round Eddie's shorter ones. Kate, still a virgin, felt that she would herself feel satisfied just with intense embrace and kissing. In her imagination, she made a momentary substitution of Rob and herself for Jess and Eddie. She had explained to Rob, shortly after they had started going out together some six months earlier, that she did not feel ready for intercourse quite yet. She had no moral objection but she had not had a regular boyfriend before. She had loved Rob all the more when he had accepted the embargo with easy good will; she appreciated his accommodatingly gentle masculinity. She had realised, though, that he had not disclosed what his own views on the matter might be.

Indeed, this issue had invited resolution when they had first moved in together, but unresolved it was to remain, at least for the time being. Still, they had each been thrilled to be living together. Kate had settled in the day before Rob arrived. She had helped him to do some basic unpacking when he came in the late afternoon. They had then walked to a local Italian restaurant and shared a large pizza and a bottle of house wine. When they had returned, Rob had come into Kate's room. He had expressed pleasure that she had made it so much her own. The wine had been exerting a gentle influence. They had stood together and embraced. Kate had felt simultaneously elated and relaxed to be held in his arms. Rob had felt her arms round his waist. He had looked down at her oval face, her blond hair and her smiling, slightly enquiring, grey eyes. She had squealed with delight when he had lifted her off the floor. At that moment, Kate had surrendered her scruples and was ready to give herself to him. She had been breathlessly excited as she became aware of his arousal and then oddly disappointed when he suddenly cut the climax short, setting her down and stepping back. He too was breathing hard, flushed in the face.

'Sorry, Katie: I…. I had forgotten what you said earlier. I was getting carried away. I didn't mean not to respect your wishes about this.'

'Oh, Rob! It's just so typically thoughtful of you to say that! But — you know — I think I may be ready now.'

Fumbling, she had started to pull up her t-shirt and unfasten her jeans at the same time.

'No. It isn't just your caution,' he had then said. 'I've got to be careful anyway. I don't want to make a mistake and hurt you- and possibly myself at the same time. I haven't mentioned it before— the situation didn't really arise — but, unlike you with boys, I have had a girlfriend before — <u>really </u>had her, if you see what I mean — but it didn't work out. I really mustn't go too far too fast — for your sake.'

He had suddenly become agitated, confused, inarticulate, in a way she had not seen before. However, the false summit which she had so exhilaratingly ascended turned from the bathos of disappointment to that of mad comedy when she saw him attempting unobtrusively to subdue his erection.

'You dear, silly boy. Tell me what happened. Who was this other girl?

She had advanced upon him.

Then, he had composed himself quickly and seized authority over the situation.

'Kate. I'd rather not talk about it. I think that I hurt some-one — almost certainly rather badly and well — I don't want to talk about it.'

'Aw, go on! Tell me! I ought to know. What was she called?'

'Her name was Lydia. And we are now going to stop this conversation.'

She had not before encountered the full strength of his will in opposition.

∼

In the kitchen at the flat, Kate had several times wanted to cook her little ready-made vegetarian meals in the microwave and offer these to Rob at the same time as Woody was untidily monopolising the room to cook his pastas which Rob had instead chosen to eat and praise.

Ironically, she felt closer to Rob when they had been visiting her mother than was proving more generally possible in the flat. Still, he now agreed with Kate's suggestion that she might make a cup of tea for them and take it into Rob's room.

'Yeah, cool. See you in a minute,' Rob said. 'I just wanna call my Dad.'

When she went into the kitchen, Woody was there amidst a field of unwashed debris. Having just returned from the ordered suburban world inhabited by her mother, and now having brushed her clean top against some tomato purée smeared on the side of one of the surfaces, Kate could contain her vexation no longer.

'Woody — you stupid fool! Look at what you've done! Look at the mess my t-shirt is in! It was new on today. Why do you have to leave everything in such a mess all the time? Don't you ever think of clearing up? What's the matter with you?'

She fought against tears.

Woody turned in surprise at Kate's outburst and was about to apologise and offer assistance when Rob entered the room.

'Look at the mess in here, Rob! And look at my new top, fresh on today!' shouted Kate.

'Oh! Kate! I'm really sorry! If you give it to me, I'll clean it up,' said Woody with genuine concern.

'I won't let you anywhere near it! You'll only wreck it completely!'

'Oh, for Heaven's sake, Katie! Don't make such a fuss! It'll wash out in one go,' interjected Rob in an even voice, smiling with surprise at the strength of her reaction.

There was a brief silence. Woody wiped the offending kitchen surface with a dish-cloth. Kate, inflamed, looked at Rob in amazement.

'You're taking his side! I can't believe I'm hearing this!'

'Aw! Don't make such a big deal of it!' continued Rob, now becoming mildly cross himself. 'The guy's apologised. What else do you want him to do? Run out onto the street and fall on his sword?'

Kate gasped.

'You two are just ganging up together. You're making it impossible to live here!'

She felt the surge of tears and ran out of the room. She sat on her bed and nursed self-pity. She felt terribly hurt. It was the first quarrel which she had had with him. How could Rob humiliate her so abruptly in front of some-one else, some-one whose characteristic carelessness had spoiled her new top, some-one who should not mean anything to Rob compared with his girl-friend? She felt stunned by the betrayal and by the way it had been so easily discharged.

After a few more sobs and a change of t-shirt, she made an effort to collect herself. Rob would be in in a moment to apologise. She would be a little stiff with him to begin with but then, when he appealed a bit more strongly, she would come round and he would love her all the more for forgiving him. This seemed a reassuring plan. She waited for the knock on the door.

It didn't come. Vexed again, Kate slipped out quietly into the hall. She could hear Rob and Woody chatting amiably in the kitchen. They were discussing football. The incident seemed to have been totally forgotten! <u>She</u> was left to suffer the indignity and inconvenience and Rob clearly couldn't care less!

Jess and Eddie emerged from Jess's room, Eddie still doing up the top button on his jeans. Jess greeted Kate and Eddie gave her a wide grin.

'All right then, Kate?' he enquired in the distorted vowels of London and a glottal omission of the hard 't's. Kate had noticed that his upper lip didn't seem to move when he spoke.

They breezed into the kitchen. Kate approached nearer but remained in the hall. No-one saw her.

'Hi you!' Jess greeted Woody. 'That smells good!'

She put her arms round him. Her long thighs extended several inches above Woody's waist. Woody offered no resistance when she bent down to kiss him.

'Hi, mate!' said Rob to Eddie as they smacked palms. 'How are your knock-kneed, bandy-legged Gunners doing? They'll be getting their usual thrashing up here in a few weeks' time!'

'How can you say that, man?' responded Eddie, smiling broadly, used by now to Rob's winding him up. 'I tell you this; you guys won't be the ones laughin' when they come up to this dump. Free-nil to Ars'nal: no question.'

'Free-nil?' repeated Rob, mimicking.

'In your dreams, mate!' said Woody, laughing, as he disentangled himself from Jess's embrace.

'How is old Arse-hole, anyway?' asked Rob, giving Eddie a friendly push as he insulted the Arsenal manager.

'Oh? Name-callin' now, are we? You guys are just such losers. You'll wonder what'll've 'it ya when our lads come!'

'Stop teasing my Eddie,' Jess demanded in good humour.

Rob yelped when she unexpectedly tickled his ribs from behind.

Kate simmered in the shadows of the hall. How could Rob continue to participate in this nonsense when he must surely know how offended and upset she, his girl-friend, must be? Why was he more interested in clowning about with this bunch than in spending time with her? She retired to her room in mortified rage.

In due course she was aware that the gathering in the kitchen had dispersed. Still no Rob. Effervescing with irritation, she went to his room and burst in without knocking.

Rob was at his desk. He could see immediately that she was angry.

'Hey! Whoa! Katie! What's up?' he asked in a tone of surprise.

"What do you mean 'What's up?' You know 'What's up!' You didn't even come to see how I was!"

'You're not still in a huff about that minor mishap to your top?' he asked and started to laugh.

'It's not funny! It might not matter to you….'

She burst into tears. He rose and made to embrace her.

'No! Don't touch me!' she shouted, almost hysterically. 'You just don't care, do you?'

He stopped in his tracks and the smile vanished.

'Well —not if you're going to go on like this! You're over-reacting ridiculously! Poor Woody....'

'Poor <u>Woody</u>!' she exclaimed. 'He's the one who caused it all! Nasty little runt!'

'No!' he countermanded, speaking with icy quietness. 'We are NOT going to start speaking about each other like that. Woody's a great guy and he's my friend. Anyone would think he'd poured the bloody stuff over you deliberately. Get a grip, for Heaven's sake! It was a minor mishap involving a little ketchup. Hundreds of thousands of people are dying of starvation in the Sudan and in Zimbabwe and you feel yourself permitted to have a strop with every-one in sight just because you've collected a stain on your top. Excuse me....'

She stopped in astonishment. She had never seen or heard him like this. But — no —she would not give in. He was making a cheap attempt to grab the moral high ground. She was furious with herself too because she couldn't stop the cascade of tears. Again, she ran out of the room.

Rob sat at his desk looking solemnly thoughtful, his lips pursed.

Woody had heard the scene and was waiting irresolutely in the Hall between their rooms. He gestured towards Kate as she rushed past. He then knocked at the door of her room. There was no reply but, when he heard her sobbing, he turned the handle and entered. He saw her sitting on her bed in a semi-foetal position. She looked at him as he came in but said nothing.

'Kate, please let me come in. I must sort this out. It's all my fault, I know.'

Woody was wearing a pair of beige shorts and a V-necked woollen jumper with light blue and grey horizontal stripes. His odd socks, one grey and one navy, had been pulled on carelessly. He was wearing no shoes. He had nothing on under his jumper, the sleeves of which were pulled up to his elbows. Kate noticed the silky brown hair on his chest, matched by a covering on his slender legs and arms and by the soft fleece fringing his handsome face. His hazel-brown eyes looked warm with gentle concern. She was about to tell him to go to Hell but, disorientated in her state of high emotion, wounded by her sharp sense of rejection and hungry for sympathy and affection, she suddenly noticed how very attractive Woody was, with his neat masculine figure so unselfconsciously presented. An unexpectedly powerful instinct prompted her not to send him away. In her confusion, she said nothing. He moved forward and sat next to her on the bed. She didn't resist when he put his arm round her shoulders. After all, wasn't this what Rob should be doing? The rain of the morning had cleared and a shaft of watery sunlight came in through the window and illuminated the hairs on Woody's bare thighs. She felt the warmth of his body against hers and suddenly yearned for the comfort he was offering. She let him consolidate his embrace and then she stroked his thigh. A part of her knew that this was dangerous and complicated but the acuteness of her self-pity conspired with the sudden compelling attractiveness of her comforter to massage her distress. As she diffidently stroked the furry surface of his thigh, his arm involuntarily pulled her gently closer.

'I hate myself for causing all this. I'll buy you a new top and get this one cleaned.'

Kate was slightly disappointed when he released her and moved himself a few inches away.

She hesitated.

'I — I'm sorry; Rob's right. I — I made too much of a fuss. It doesn't matter really.'

'No — you've every right to be mad at me. It's typical. I'm always doing things like this. I'm always annoying my Mum and my sisters because I'm such a mess. I'm just hopeless.'

The palpably ingenuous charm of his self-abasement had a magical effect on Kate. She couldn't help laughing at him.

'Oh, Woody — you're such a sweet boy; I didn't realise. I judged too quickly. I'm sorry.'

He got up. She remained sitting on the bed, smiling now through her moist eyes.

'So- am I forgiven? I _will_ sort this out- like I said. Please don't be upset.'

'Of course — I feel such a silly! I feel quite ashamed.'

''And I'm not really 'a nasty little runt'?''

'Oh — Woody! Oh —you must have heard!'

'Well — you _were_ shouting,' he said, smiling.

'Oh, I'm so ashamed. I'm so sorry!'

'I know I'm small but I hope I'm not nasty!'

'Of course you aren't. I only realise now what a dear, sweet boy you are. Oh God, I've really made a mess of this!'

Kate leapt up from the bed and, rushing up to Woody, embraced him, once again giving way to tears.

'Hey! Come on!' he said gently, as he held her. 'I didn't want to upset you again. It's all-right, Kate. It's OK!'

He held her tightly as she put her arms round him and, quite spontaneously, kissed him at precisely the moment when Rob walked into the room.

FOUR

'It's not like that, Rob. It's not what you're thinking at all.'

'Oh — excuse me for getting it wrong! I go into my girl-friend's room to find her locked in embrace with one of my best friends, at the moment when she's planting a kiss on his lips, and I'm wrong to feel pissed off about it and then I'm to be blamed for misinterpreting the fucking obvious! Oh — silly, wicked me! Of course, it's all <u>my</u> fault 'cos I'm the dumb-arse having nasty suspicious wrong thoughts! Sorree!'

'I know what it must look like…..'

'Too right!'

'But you know me well enough….'

'Do I? I'm not so sure!'

'You <u>know</u> I'm not the sort of guy to go behind your back and try to make up to your girl-friend.'

They were alone in the kitchen. Rob had pursued Woody there after the latter had succeeded in making a hasty exit from Kate's room. Woody had given an honest account of events but Rob was not persuaded.

Katie now came in; she was in a state of obvious trepidation. She had overheard the predictable exchange between the two boys. She was nervous and concerned but felt, for once, that she might be able to exercise some control over the situation. She advanced upon Rob as if to hug him.

'Woody's right, Rob. He just came in to console me.'

'Oh, I see! That's why you were all over him, kissing him on his mouth, with your arms round him.'

'No - Rob…..'

Defeated again, the look of distress returned.

'I'm sorry, Kate! I'm sick of this. It's one thing after another. It's gone too far.'

He turned on his heel and left the room.

'And I don't want either of you coming after me with another load of bull-shit!'

Kate crumpled. She was standing between Woody and the door. He stood irresolutely.

'Oh Woody!' she sobbed.

He was sorry for her and he still felt guilty about the tomato purée. He didn't resist when, once again, she collapsed into him. Kate felt his fleecy beard against her face and his arms round her waist and she felt more than comfort. Instinctively, she put her arms round him.

~

Academe imposed its will on Monday morning. Woody set off early to go his laboratory. Rob, while avoiding his friend, also left the house early to work in the library before meeting up with some other friends to kick a football around for a bit in the afternoon. He came back quietly and slipped into his room to start the week's essay. Then he left the house again to attend an unofficial old school reunion which he and a few friends had previously organised at Pizza Express in the city centre. Halfway through the afternoon, Kate, still deeply upset, took the 45 to Cheadle Hulme. She longed for her mother's wisdom and support but, as the bus waited at the interminable East Didsbury traffic lights, she realised that her pride would make any disclosure about the quarrel too hard to bear. Also, it would be too bad if her mother took against Rob and he became less welcome at the house. Moreover, as the bus slowly lurched across the indecipherable boundary artificially separating the metropolitan boroughs of

Manchester and Stockport, Kate realised that she was thinking about Woody more than Rob. It was scruffy little Woody's image that persisted in her mind's eye, his carelessly shaven face fixed in an expression of guileless earnestness. She had heard Jess calling him 'sweet' and considered that that was just about right.

∼

Rob's reaction to the quarrel was more dangerous than either Kate or Woody might reasonably have understood. His bright, outgoing, wide-ranging personality was disinclined to let perceived injustices or offences fester. He would be the first to condemn disloyalty, in himself as well as others, but his ability to ignore or transform setbacks combined with a decisive nature and a clarity of purpose which enabled him ruthlessly to delete unwelcome incidents or issues from his life. He was most certainly upset for the rest of that Sunday. He had loved Kate for her undeniable prettiness, her gentleness and her intelligent seriousness. He liked her particular representation of suburban Manchester, with her flat, slurred vowels and her humble, innocent, wide-eyed sense of a metropolitan existence just beyond the margins. He had loved her for her vulnerability. His own circumstances enabled him to feel a ready empathy for the little family, maimed by the tragic loss of its father and husband. The neat little semi-detached house in Cheadle Hulme was a novelty which he cherished, with its tidy little garden, its tastefully conventional prints of famous pictures, its china cabinet full of nick-knacks, its net curtains. He respected the quiet courage of Mrs Braithwaite, always immaculately presented, not without a studiously considered dash of imagination, ever keen to welcome him and relate to his own concerns.

When, however, he woke early on the Monday morning, true to his nature, Rob felt that he had to take stock of the situation. He couldn't just bumble along with it and yesterday's events could not be ignored. He had suddenly seen Kate in a different light. He had already recognised an amber light when, to his surprise, she had made no effort to relate to Woody and Jess and he did not welcome the clinging domesticity which, rather too bossily, she had been attempting to dictate. He had been irritated once when he had returned to the house to find that she had been through his socks and his shirts, and even his boxer shorts, and arranged them all with a ludicrous neatness which he had no intention of maintaining. If there is now anything between her and Woody, he thought, with grim amusement, let her try that sort of nonsense with him! Also, he had quickly given up the effort of tactfully refusing her tedious microwave vegetarian meals. In that regard, the presence of Woody had proved a Godsend. He had been annoyed by the scene she had indulged in over the incident in the kitchen yesterday and then genuinely shocked by the spectacle which he had so suddenly come across in her room with Woody. He had seen the look on her face and the nature of the kiss and it had revealed a duplicity of nature and a surrender to appetite which, he was absolutely clear, he was not willing to put up with. And so he decided that, although today, Monday, he would keep himself away from the immediate heat of the situation, when Kate did come to him, as he knew she would, he would tell her, with as little drama and unpleasantness as possible, that there was to be no future in their relationship.

With regard to Woody, he was not quite so sure. He was inclined to believe that his feckless, warm-hearted, well-meaning friend was telling the truth. The expression on Woody's face when Kate had rushed upon him had been one of slightly puzzled, embarrassed uncertainty. It would be typical of Woody to want to try to help and then become hopelessly enmeshed and morally blackmailed within the emotional storm and wily machinations of Kate's instability. Rob thought that he might let that one ride. He would be less matey with Woody for the time being. If Kate really got her bourgeois little claws into his relatively defenceless being, there could be little future in the friendship. If not, things might come back together again; Rob hoped that they would. Thus resolved, he took a shower, dressed, grabbed a cereal bar, and left the house, focused on the day ahead.

Kate was the first one back to Didsbury that evening. She returned after having had high tea with her mother. Woody returned late after meeting up with some mates for a few drinks following his day's work in the laboratory. Rob returned even later. Kate's heart pounded as she heard him coming in. Nervous though she was, she wanted the confrontation over. Now, she just wanted him to forgive her; she would take all the blame. He was bound to knock at her door and offer either reconciliation or rebuke. Even the latter would be better than nothing, especially as she had decided that she would accept it. But he went straight to his room and shut the door. Once again, she felt acute self-pity and, within half an hour, her earlier sense of remorse had turned back to anger. How dare he treat her like this? He'd obviously decided to break it all off - just like that! He was enjoying hurting her; he didn't care. Her mind turned to the possible comfort available from Woody next-door. She thought of him in his little shorts looking worried for her. Jess did not come back at all that night. Staying over at Eddie's, she did not need to dream about boys. She had Eddie fast in her arms, her long legs securing him as she relaxed into a post-coital sleep.

Kate continued to feel troubled the next day. She had not raised the matter with her mother yesterday. They had spent some of the time going through a large cupboard which Mara had preferred not to tackle on her own.

The process had had its sad moments and they had both shed occasional tears. Today, she sat, abstracted, through two lectures in the morning and a seminar in the late afternoon. By chance, the latter entirely comprised people with whom she had not been taught last year. She had not taken much trouble to get to know them because she had felt so intensely committed to Rob that she had wanted to spend all her spare time and energy with him. She left as soon as she could and caught a crowded number 45 to take her back to Didsbury.

The flat was empty. Rob had stayed in town and was going to the cinema with two of the friends he had shared a meal with last night. Jess had taken her work back to Eddie's place. She was sitting in an armchair in Eddie's tiny room in Fallowfield, managing to get through a substantial section of Proust by raising her eyes every few sentences to take in the full wonder of Eddie in his white rugby kit as he worked on his laptop on his desk.

Kate tried to work but found it impossible. The computer screen was before her, sclerotic with lifeless data which she was too distracted to assimilate. She gave up and downloaded her e-mail for the first time for several days. It indicated various messages, sent by her old school friends on Facebook. She entered the social networking site and read the messages on her 'wall'. Now, she wondered if she had been right to stay in

Manchester. The original reason had been the presence of all her friends but they had chosen to go elsewhere and, when she looked up their home pages on Facebook, they were all making exciting new friendships in Bristol or Nottingham or Newcastle. The photographs all depicted happy parties, jolly new boyfriends, groups of friends eating and smiling together in restaurants. The most recent message was from her friend, Pippa, in Leeds:-

'Write you cow! What's the matter with you?'

A few days earlier Pippa had written:-

'Hi! How's you? How's life back in old Mcr? Looked up your photos. Really like the hot boyfriend! How you get hold of him? He's gorgeous! Must meet him when I'm next over! Don't worry! Only joking! Had a girls' get-together with Ellie and Steph. Talked about you, hope your ears were burning. Ha ha! Have you seen what Harriet's got her claws into at Durham? Not bad, huh? Look up that photo where she's legless and sitting on his knee. Poor guy! Ha ha! It's still a bit on-off with Freddie; we'll have to see. Lol. Write — or text!'

The invitation was on the screen to 'write something.' Kate became nostalgic. She thought of all the happy laughs she had enjoyed with Pippa, Ellie, Steph and Harriet. Kate had been useless at lacrosse but it had all been such crazy fun as they had bent double with bottled up laughter at the sight of Miss Probert powering across the pitch, her florid face demonic with commitment, 200 pounds of propelled energy ready to fell anybody in its path, including, one afternoon, skinny little Mr Coussins, who had inexplicably appeared, wearing a pair of navy shorts which, to the lasting amusement of the girls, revealed his bony knees and hairy legs. He was one of the very few male members of staff and, fresh out of university, easily the teacher with the least effective classroom control.

She remembered the hilarious notes that had passed to and fro during the boring R.S. lessons with Mrs Dunford and the times they had nearly burst with suppressed mirth in French with Mademoiselle Leroux, who repeated, with a degree of disgust only available to a Frenchwoman, *'Oh la la! Quel triste temps aujourd'hui, mes enfants! Quel triste temps!'* every time it rained which, in Manchester, was a not infrequent occurrence. There was that moment when Holly Davies had been giving a passable, if exaggerated, imitation, unaware that Mademoiselle Leroux had entered the room. Mademoiselle's pencilled eyebrows had nearly disappeared above the top of her forehead, *'Alors! 'Ollee! Qu'est ce que tu fais? 'Que dis-tu? Quoi?'* Holly had gone as red as a tomato as she stammered, 'Sorry, Miss! No, it was nothing! I was just being silly.' *'Eh bien! Tout le monde a le devoir? Non?'* Mademoiselle had glided on to the readily available threat with impressive frostiness.

Kate started to type into the inviting box at the top of the screen.

'Hi, Pippa! OMG — I miss you and the others! I'm not sure it was the right thing to do to stay here. Just had a horrid row with the 'hot' boyfriend and frankly I think he sucks. Might chuck him over. Specially as there's this cute little guy living here too- pretty and really sweet. Might see if he's available. Called Woody. Actually, his real name's Chris but everybody calls him Woody. Since the row with Rob, I quite fancy Woody. Work's soooo boring! Think I made a mistake doing Psychology. Oh well! Lol (for you anyway — sob,sob!).'

She hit the 'Send' box. Then she froze. Oh my God! Rob was a regular user of Facebook and it was quite possible that Woody was on it too. Rob will almost certainly go to her page next time he signs on. It'll appear on his wall anyway. And what about Woody? Oh- why is everything going wrong? There was no deleting these cringe-making messages unless you did it immediately and, given Rob's current mood, the consequences could be quite awful. And she had probably screwed up with Woody now too, and that, she realised, mattered to her quite a lot.

She accessed Rob's wall on Facebook. The recent messages on his wall in both directions exclusively concerned the meeting with his old school pals the previous evening: who could come, who couldn't, choosing the restaurant, who would book (it was Rob), which bar they would meet in first: on and on it went: terse young men's messages of arrangement, interspersed with occasional swipes of jocular obscenity.

She discovered, through the 'Find Friends' facility, that Woody was also on Facebook. She quickly went on to see that he had not used the network for months: typical Woody! Let's hope he didn't start looking at it now! Under 'interests', Woody had recorded 'ManU, socialising, cooking (mainly pasta — come and buy some!), cutting up defenceless little insects (to annoy Animal Rights Protesters), women (I s'pose….)'.

Woody's entry slightly alleviated her misery; she even managed a little smile. She tried to type a message of recantation to Rob but every attempt looked more absurdly unconvincing than the last one. She gave up. She intuitively sensed Rob's capacity to wield the axe but still tried to escape from the dismal conclusion that their relationship might be over. It had all happened with such terrifying speed. Or had it? She began to realise that she had not heeded previous warnings, like their different attitudes to the other two members of the ménage, her obtuse failure to realise that Rob didn't share her rather feminine tastes (and quantities!) in food, his demonstrations of patience when she had complained about not seeing him for half a day, and so on. But she didn't want to lose him. He had meant so much to her.

To begin with, she had not been able to believe her luck in landing such a conquest but, as they had got to know each other ever better, she really had come to love him for much, much more than his appearance and his charm. What an irretrievable disaster it all was now!

She heard Woody coming into the house and up the stairs. He went into his room. Kate sent a few further messages to her friends on Facebook, taking care not to mention either Rob or Woody. When she heard Woody go into the kitchen, she too got up. He gave her a friendly open smile.

'No tomato purée today — and, look, I've tidied up!'

Kate felt a surge of affection. How gentle he was — how 'sweet'! Even before the quarrel, Rob had always been the boss, masterfully deciding what they might do together, and she had willingly bowed to his enterprise and initiative.

'Woody, that's wonderful! It looks great!'

As Kate beamed at him, she was amused by today's version of Woody scruffiness. He was wearing a light blue shirt, with a collar so worn that it had split at the back, and a pair of black chino cotton trousers, spattered with mud, with the hems frayed and a ragged tear down the side of one of the legs.

Woody saw Kate looking him up and down.

'Yeah — I'm a really scruffy little guy, I know,' he smiled ruefully.

Kate found him irresistibly lovable in his vulnerability and good intentions; she felt intensely protective towards him.

'Oh, Woody! You're a lovely boy! I've only just realised how much in the last few days. But you've got to do something about those trousers. You can't go round the place like that!'

'I think I've got a safety pin somewhere. I'll look for it.'

'That's no good! Have you ever washed them?'

Woody smiled shyly and went slightly pink.

'Right! Get them off! I'm going to wash them NOW! Then I'm going to sew that rip and tidy up the hems. We can't have you looking such a complete wreck!'

'I'll go and put something else on; I'll put them in the machine myself later.'

'No- you know you won't! Take them off now and I'll do it.'

He hesitated, looking slightly embarrassed and faintly incredulous.

'Go on!' she bossed. 'I'm going to do <u>something</u> to help you to look half decent! And that shirt's had it! How long have you been wearing it?'

He shrugged his shoulders and spread his hands out.

'Well! Anyway! Get those chinos off! Here! Now! I'm not letting you escape! And that shirt! At least we'll have it clean, even if then it has to be thrown out.'

Embarrassed but also somewhat amused by the situation, and seldom one to refuse when under duress, he complied.

'My boxer shorts <u>are</u> clean on today!' he affirmed, colouring again as Kate briskly took the offending garments from him and he stood in the middle of the kitchen in a pair of white Calvin Kleins and short black socks, the left one of which sported a conspicuous hole revealing his big toe.

'I'm going to show you how to use this washing machine,' insisted Kate, quickly thinking up a ploy to keep him in the room.

Although Woody was much more technically proficient than Kate, he humoured her. Kate's mood altered dramatically at the sight of a half-naked Woody. She quickly put the powder into the machine and started the programme. Then she stepped towards him and, once again, hugged him.

'Woody — you're such a sweet boy! I doubt if you've got any idea….'

He stood uncomfortably in receipt of her attentions. When she started to kiss him, however, he resisted. Without pushing her away, he managed to disengage himself.

'No, Kate, this is going too far and it's not right!'

She was surprised and slightly nettled.

'Don't you like me Woody? Rob seemed to find me attractive.'

The enquiry was made with slight anxiety.

'Of course you're an attractive girl; there's no doubt about that. Please don't think I think otherwise. But I've got to be loyal to Rob. He's a very special friend. I've already managed to annoy him once and I don't like antagonising him.'

'You're not scared of him surely?' asked Kate flirtatiously.

'That's not fair,' Woody replied politely. 'No, I'm not, but I don't want to hurt him and I want to protect my friendship with him. You and I mustn't hug and kiss. Really not, you know!' He gave her a kind smile.

'I don't care what Rob thinks. I'm through with him. I'm fed up with him deciding everything for everybody and bossing everybody about. Woody, I didn't realise what a sweet boy you were until the other day — and you're so attractive — especially in your underwear,' she giggled.

He made as if to leave the room but her last observation caused him to pause.

'It is funny us having this conversation with you not having any trousers on,' laughed Kate. She felt that she would do anything to keep him with her.

'Kate, you've got to stop this. I'm not going on with it. I'm loyal to Rob. And you should be too. One little disagreement shouldn't wreck your relationship. He's a great guy! Give it another go!'

'No, Woody. I want a relationship with you now. But since that's not to be, I'll be a single girl again.'

'Go back to Rob!' he said more loudly, smiling.

'When the drying cycle's finished, I'll sew your trousers and hand them in.'

'I'll make sure you don't find me like this!' he concluded, gesturing to his underwear.

FIVE

KATE RETURNED TO THE FLAT the following afternoon. Again, all the others were out. She felt lonely and ill used. She was unhappy now when her fellow flatmates were present and felt miserably isolated when they were not. She worked perfunctorily for a bit on an assignment but the once scrupulously conscientious schoolgirl was becoming a disenchanted student. She now wished that she had chosen a different subject and another university. It did not occur to her that a similar situation might just as easily occur elsewhere: that, although the place might be different, she would be much the same.

She got up from her desk and noticed Woody's chinos lying over a chair. She picked them up and hugged them, freshly scented and clean, as a result of their one and only experience in the washing machine. She set up the ironing board in the kitchen and pressed them carefully. Then, back in her room, she found her sewing kit (given to her by Auntie Jane two years or so back) and carefully stitched the rip through the cotton cloth on the left leg of the garment.

All the time, she was silently lamenting her unhappiness. She felt wounded by Woody's rejection, fearful of Rob's anger, faintly jealous of Jesse's apparently successful worldliness, lonely at the thought of all her Manchester girl-friends having a good time in other, apparently exotic, universities, and then, spiralling downwards, she realised how much she missed her father, who, in his quiet, thoughtfully indulgent, way, would sense just when to proffer the proverbial shoulder upon which to weep. She thought of her mother too but even Kate, in her self-absorbed sorrow, sustained the inbuilt decency which sensed that it would be wrong to add to her mother's grief, sustained so heroically, by imposing that of her own. Moreover, even if it was motivated by pride, she wanted her mother to think that she could stand on her own two feet.

The sewing completed, she pressed the now beloved garment to her face, using it to wipe away a few tears, and took it to Woody's room. She knew that he was out but knocked first just in case. She had never actually been inside the room since Woody had occupied it. It was dark because Woody had not pulled the curtains before leaving that morning. She switched the light on and met the chaos with incredulity. The jumble of jeans, t-shirts, boxer shorts, socks, pullovers, trainers, books, ring folders, letters still in their ripped open envelopes, half used packets of biscuits, empty beer cans, newspapers, cracked plastic ballpoint pens, notepads, computer print-outs, CDs, cans of deodorant spray, football shorts and so on which littered the entire room- on the floor, on the desk, on the chairs, on the bed- was so total and so random that, Kate thought, if, ironically, one were to design chaos, one could not have done the job more effectively.

She stood, with the neatly pressed and repaired chinos over her arm. She did not know where to put them. It seemed wrong simply to drop them arbitrarily, in their new, pristine respectability, into a disordered mess which would engulf them. She pulled the curtains and decided that the only thing possible was to do some tidying up. She decided to make a start by moving everything off the bed and, having tidied up the duvet and the pillow, she placed the chinos at the top of the bed and gradually classified Woody's other clothes into neat piles which she lay out across it. She matched up scattered pairs of socks and folded shirts, underclothes and jeans. She quickly filled the bin with rubbish. She stacked papers and books on Woody's desk. The point came where there was little more that she could do. Still, she thought, it was a definite improvement. If only Woody would let her love him, she would soon organise his sweet, docile, untidy maleness. But, the melancholy thought could not be dispelled; it was something else which was not to be. She found a pen which worked and the back of an empty envelope, and wrote him a gentle note to say that she had repaired his trousers and done a little tidying up.

She returned disconsolately to her room and sat in front of her computer. She called up Facebook. She entered Woody's name but he had not yet checked her application to become one of her 'friends' and so she was denied access to his photo's. She then typed in Rob's name but, instead of flashing up Rob's home page, nothing happened. She clicked the mouse on her own list of friends, only to discover that Rob had removed himself from it, thus denying her access to him. She was shocked by the swift and calculated brutality of the rebuff. She had never experienced so sharp a rejection before. She let out a little cry of distress and found a tissue to catch newly generated tears. She was beyond either feeling anger or submitting herself to self-criticism. She felt engulfed by a rising tide of despair. Lonely and afraid, Katie could think of nothing positive to relieve her current plight. She wanted to be a little girl again, playing on her own in the sunny garden of her home, loved by both her doting parents. She looked at the familiar teddy on her bed, here in the now strangely adult hostility of this anonymous student flat, and remembered her imaginary conversations with him back in her childhood past. Then there were the dolls having a tea-party on a rug on the grass, her mother and her Auntie Jane suggesting routine domestic activities possibly engaged in by the fictitious, plastic family. The memory surged back of the moment when her father, suddenly lifting her off the ground and, holding her in his arms, had said,

'Oh! My little girl! Your Mummy and Daddy love you *so* much!' and the feeling of total happiness and security in which at that moment she had reposed.

She had loved it when, each weekday evening, her father had returned from work and, after embracing her mother, had again picked her up when she had run towards him, asking with his big smile,

'And how has my little girl been today? What has my Katie been doing?'

She recalled the occasions when her Mummy and Daddy had stood together, laughing on cue at her childish antics.

No more. Instead, she was confronted by the icily adult fury of the first boy whom she had really loved, trusted and depended on, and the gently reproving rejection of the next. She sat on her bed, rocking to and fro, with her teddy in her arms, not really able to consider that she had, perhaps unconsciously, expected these attractive, self-possessed young men to fulfil the dual roles of lover and father. Now, in her extreme self-pity and sense of total loss, she found blame, with its minatory finger pointing unequivocally at herself. She realised that there was no going back with Rob and she viewed the final seal of his impending rejection, when they inevitably met face to face, with something not far short of terror. And she had made a fool of herself with Woody, appearing like the slut which, surely, to be fair, she never was. She knew that Woody's detachment from her, enforced so gently but so firmly yesterday, was equally irrecoverable.

She returned to her desk and wrote another note to Woody:-

Dearest Woody,
I'm really sorry I behaved so badly. I can't imagine what I was thinking of and, even worse, I can't imagine what you must now be thinking of me. Please try to forget all that I ever said. I'm quite hopeless,
Love, Kate.

She hurried back to his room and put the note beside the earlier one, making a point of not being distracted by the limitless opportunities available for further clearing up.

Now, she decided to text Rob:-

'u deleted me from fb. I don't blame u. I love u Rob and I'm terribly sorry. Please try to forgive me even tho I don't deserve it. XXX.'

She could not settle. She returned to Facebook. She called up Pippa's photo's. There was a sequence of Pippa in embrace with her boyfriend, Freddie, also from Manchester. They looked blissfully happy and, slightly, engagingly, naughty at the same time. And yet, was this what it was really like? The photo's had been added to Pippa's Profile page some weeks ago and the 'on-off' remark in her friend's message might euphemistically be covering feelings not entirely different from her own current distress.

Curiosity prompted her to look up Harriet in Durham and see for herself what her other friend had 'got her claws into', as Pippa had so bluntly described. She was quickly able to see what Pippa meant. There was Harriet, leggy, with long blond hair, wearing skinny jeans, her breasts alluringly supported by a tight-fitting red top, her midriff exposed, a glass of white wine in her right hand as she turned to face the camera, her left arm round the waist of a stunningly handsome young man, tall and slim, and also fair, with vividly sparkling blue eyes, wearing a blue and white short-sleeved checked shirt and a pair of jeans, his right arm round Harriet's shoulder. Kate thought that they appeared very much in love, Harriet looking the part which she, Kate, had so recently failed to be in her dealing with Rob. She discovered that the photo's had been tagged: Harriet Mottershead and Guy Tilney-Smith. Kate thought that the name seemed appropriate to the boy's picture. She wondered if he might have been at the same public school as Rob: probably not: there were so many.

She heard some-one entering the house. She realised immediately that the briskness of movement indicated that it was Rob. She quashed the automatic impulse to get up and hurry out to meet him. She sat in irresolute panic. She wondered whether or not he had checked the text so recently sent and, if so, if he had just deleted it. Although her own mobile was switched on, she checked the messages; there were none.

Less than ten minutes later, she heard his door opening. She rushed out to confront him. He was wearing his tracksuit and setting off for a run. She tried to stand in front of him.

'Rob! Rob, did you get my text?'

He ignored her, his dark eyes tinged with irritation and contempt, and brusquely pushed past, running down the stairs and leaving the house, slamming the front door behind him.

Kate, now deeply agitated again, could not bear to go back into her empty room. She had to sort this out. She knew Rob's route for his regular runs. He would follow Wilmslow Road, run through Didsbury 'Village', cross the playing fields opposite the Fletcher Moss Museum and, reaching the tow-path on the bank of the Mersey, follow it north, returning along Ford Lane back into Didsbury. If she was quick, she could set off into Didsbury, turn directly into Ford Lane and intercept him somewhere along the tow-path. She would *not* let him pass until they had put this awful quarrel behind them. She would take all the blame; after all, as she now considered, she was really the one primarily at fault.

She hurried down Wilmslow Road, passing the neatly inscrutable suburban houses, set back from the pavement, behind gardens tidied for the approaching winter. A number 45 swished past. She passed the library and the police station, crossing the road at the busy junction with Barlow Moor Road and, as the increasingly chic Didsbury shops began, she turned right down Ford Lane. She soon reached the tow-path which ran along the eastern bank of the Mersey and, knowing that she was now almost certain to meet up with Rob coming the opposite way, she relaxed her pace as she followed it south. She rehearsed what she was going to say; it would be total surrender but she had to make it convincing; she so wanted him back. No-one was around, apart from a couple of disappearing golfers on the other side of the river. The fawn coloured river was unusually turbulent after the week-end's heavy rain as it flowed swiftly past in noiseless anger, confined within banks artificially raised and strengthened by interfering man. Fewer than fifty miles to the west, it would emerge into the Irish Sea as the mighty estuary responsible for the creation of the great port of Liverpool. The scene was grey under a lowering sky. The landscape was flat and featureless, the sodden golf links extending to the west and the decayed, late Autumn, remnants of thick, uncultivated vegetation to her left, growing to a sufficient height to obscure any prospect beyond, despite the path running along a substantial levée.

Some minutes later, she saw him approaching her. As he had not been expecting this, she had surprise on her side. She felt her heart racing and all thought of her planned remarks left her head. She saw Rob hesitate when he noticed her, and, for one desperate moment, she thought that he might be about to turn round and run back in the opposite direction. However, she quickly corrected any such delusion, even before he continued ahead, realising how alien it would be to his nature to retreat from any situation.

When they met, he shook his head and raised the palms of his hands, moving them forward, to indicate the pointlessness of the encounter which she had manipulated. Before Kate could issue any opening words of penance, he, confounding her plan, spoke sternly into the damp air,

'This is pointless, Kate. It's no use. Let's just agree to make a complete break of it and then, after the heat of it all has died down, we might be able to see ourselves as friends but, honestly, nothing more.'

Rob's breathlessness, so immediately after his physical exertion, exacerbated the harshness of his tone.

'Oh, Rob! Please! I'm really sorry!' she wailed.

Now they were standing face to face and he had had time to catch his breath.

'So 'sorry' that you were happy to write in public on Facebook that you think your 'boyfriend sucks' (have I got the right, elegant, use of language?) and that you 'might chuck him over.''

'That was a mistake…..'

'You bet it was!'

'That's not how I feel; it was a silly mistake! I was just angry at the moment I wrote it.'

'I can't be bothered with all this, Kate! We're through! Please just get that into your head!'

He set off to run past her. She blocked his way and put her arms round his waist. In a flood of tears, she appealed to him,

'Oh Rob! It was an idiotic thing to do! It's not the way I feel at all. I'll write on my 'wall' again and tell every-one how much I love you….'

'If you could just hear yourself! You're so childish! Now, get off me and just let me past!'

As she clung onto him, he wrenched her free and pushed her out of the way. Kate lost her footing on the slippery path and, with a little shriek of alarm, she fell into the Mersey.

Rob stood, transfixed with shock. By the time he was able to make any movement at all, Kate's head was bobbing above the river's seething surface twenty metres downstream. He ripped off his trainers and tracksuit and dived into the freezing, agitated water in his underclothes. He was swept along at a furious speed but could not now even see Kate. Indeed, although Rob was a strong swimmer, all he could do was fight with the eddies and swirls of conflicting currents just enough to keep his own head above the water. The sharp stab of the icy water quickly overpowered him into a paralysis of numbness. He had no independent power of movement at all. The next thing he knew was to find himself in violent collision with a low muddy outcrop of the bank. He heard a shout above him and, as he instinctively brought his right arm up, his wrist was seized and he was hauled roughly up the bank. He saw himself gazing first at the beer belly and then at the shaved bullet head of a six foot three, 250 pound man in his mid-thirties.

'Are you all-right mate? I thawt you was a raat gonner! I were joost passin'. You was bloody looky that fookin' river swept you int' bank….'

Rob's rescuer spoke with the rough 'r's and flat, unvaried vowels of the south Manchester housing estates.

'My girlfriend! Kate! She's fallen in! I was trying to save her! We've got to get her out!'

The shaved head looked left and right along the river but could see nothing. He held the drenched and shivering Rob tightly but effortlessly in his powerful, hairless, tattooed arms to prevent him from collapsing onto the ground. As Rob passed out, the man called 999 on his mobile.

SIX

'How are you now then, luvvie?'

Rob had been awake for a little time, after coming round from the sedative following his arrival in the ambulance at the A&E Department of the hospital.

The kind nurse was older than most of her colleagues and assumed a motherly aspect.

'Are you comfy enough? Let me just raise these pillows for you. Now that you're awake, I expect that you might like to sit up for a bit.'

As she arranged the pillows, Rob levered himself up. He had worked out that he was in hospital shortly after coming round but, for a time, the previous hours of his life, even when he had been conscious, had been blanked out of his memory. He had lain there feeling disembodied but uneasy as he drifted in and out of consciousness. Then, suddenly, the horror of the immediate past had come rushing towards him, released by his subconscious.

'Katie!' he had suddenly called out. 'Oh, my God! What's happened?'

This had alerted the nurse who had now come across to his bedside.

'Katie! My girlfriend! She fell into the river! What's happened to her?'

'I don't know luv. You've been brought in because you had fallen in the river yourself.'

'But….'

'Now, I'm just going to get you a nice cup of tea. There's a gentleman here who's been waiting to speak to you. He's from the police. You were involved in an accident at the river.'

'But KATIE! HOW IS SHE?'

'I don't know, luvvie, but this gentleman might be able to tell you more while I get you that cuppa.'

A young uniformed police constable had now also appeared and, as the nurse left, he sat down on the chair beside the bed. He was tall and slim, with short dark hair and kindly humorous brown eyes, set in a face made handsome by its regular bone structure. He was wearing a short-sleeved blue shirt above the dark trousers of his uniform. He smiled encouragingly as he looked down at Rob while bending down to take his seat.

'I've told the policeman that you must stop if you get tired, luv. He understands.'

'I'm desperate to go to the loo. I — I'm sorry.'

Rob had suddenly felt the discomfort as his faculties returned.

'Of course, luvvie. I'll just take you to where it is. I think that it's best that we try to get you moving. Then I'll get you that tea and I'll pull the screen round your bed for privacy when you get back. Ooh, look at you! You're fine, aren't you? Just a few cuts and bruises to be dressed again and the doctor's going to keep you in overnight in case there's been any delayed concussion.'

Both she and the policeman had to steady Rob momentarily when he got out of bed. His legs temporarily gave way and he felt disorientated. He noticed that he had been dressed in a white smock which came to just below his knees. There was a bandage round his right fore-arm and a dressing held by surgical tape on his right shin; that leg was feeling rather sore. As he got up, the lingering sedative made him feel slightly muzzy again.

When Rob had settled back in bed again and had relished a few sips of comforting, hot, sweet tea, P.C. Hamer made a gentle start:-

'Rob, I'm P.C. Hamer. Call me by my first name, Stuart. Now, try to remember; tell me exactly what happened on the river bank.'

'But Katie! How is she? I keep asking. They don't seem to know.'

'You don't know?'

'No.'

'Give me your hand, Mate.'

Rob did so and, fully alert now, looked Stuart in the eye.

'God, what's happened?'

'I'm afraid it's bad news, Rob. Katie drowned after falling in the river this afternoon.'

Rob withdrew his hand abruptly and sat upright.

'No! O God! No!'

'I'm afraid so. I'm really very sorry.'

'I jumped in to try to save her but the current was too strong. Oh — if only I could have reached her! Is it definite that she's ….she's….?'

His voice faltered.

'I'm afraid so, Rob. She was found further downstream and identified.'

'No! No! No!'

Rob burst into tears and covered his face with his hands.

Hearing the noise, the nurse came back. Rob was given a further mild sedative.

Stuart said that, if he may, he would wait by the bedside until Rob had recovered sufficiently to tell more.

After about fifteen minutes, Rob seemed able to explain what happened. But it was garbled. He was very upset and, indeed, he was confused as he tried to put those dreadful few seconds into any sort of clear order. Sobs and words competed for articulacy. He now remembered more clearly the argument between them but he could not bear to include it in his account. He suddenly felt wracked by guilt but he couldn't allow such a shadow to defile any public statement of their last moments together.

P.C. Hamer had not expected to be the one to break the news of Katie's death. He was himself only a few years older than Rob. He felt deeply sympathetic. He considered that it might have just as easily been his own girlfriend, Karen. It seemed clear what Rob was trying to say. He did his best to write an accurate version in his notebook and, gently asking Rob if he could bear to listen to it, read it back to him.

'This isn't official, Rob. And, anyway, we're talking about death by misadventure so, obviously, it's not like a criminal investigation. There's likely to be a coroner's inquest and so there might need to be a formal statement made later on which, if you agree with what it says, you could sign. But you've enough to worry about without needing to bother with that now.'

The policeman read out his attempt at putting together Rob's version of the tragic event.:-

'Robert Hadfield left the premises (which he shared with Kate Braithwaite and two other students) at approximately 4pm on Tuesday 28 October and set off for a run, passing through Didsbury and approaching the tow-path on the east side of the River Mersey after passing Fletcher Moss; he then started to run in a northerly direction. He met his girl-friend, Kate Braithwaite, shortly afterwards on

the tow-path. The path was slippery after recent rain. As they embraced, she lost her footing and fell into the river which was swollen, again as the result of recent rain. Robert stripped to his underwear and jumped into the river in an attempt to save Kate but the current was too strong and he was swept back into the bank where he was rescued by Wayne Shaw who was walking southwards along the tow-path.'

Exact addresses were included. P.C. Hamer explained again that this summary was not official and that, if he felt it necessary, Rob could correct or refine it later when his head was clearer and the worst of the shock might be behind him.

'Did Kate usually walk out to meet you when you went on a run, Rob?'

'No, it was the first time.'

'Any particular reason for that?'

P.C. Hamer smiled gently, making it clear that he was not necessarily expecting an answer.

'No- No, not so far as I can think of, anyway,' hesitated Rob, his face beginning to crumple with renewed distress.

'No, of course not, Rob. There doesn't have to be, after all.'

The nurse returned and hovered meaningfully. P.C. Hamer took his leave, wishing Rob well.

Rob slid back down into the bed to lie flat, his head upon the pillow. He started to worry about the accuracy of the statement. What he had said was not the whole truth and it was quite possible that the whole tragedy might not have occurred if he had not pushed Kate out of his way. However, he did not want the world to know that their relationship had ended in such acrimony. He felt wretched about it. The poor girl's very last action had been to try to reconcile them. His thoughts spiralled downwards as he considered that he had rejected this and (he now deliberated with intensifying horror) had quite possibly been responsible for her death.

His father arrived a few hours later. He was deeply concerned and had booked into a hotel for the night. He kept pressing for exact information about the incident- more so than P.C. Hamer had done.

Rob found it easier to cope when Woody, Jess and Eddie visited together.

'Eddie insisted on bringing you these stupid grapes,' said Jess.

'Woman — it's what yer do when some-one's in 'ospital, like; don't ya know that?' ' responded Eddie, his London accent assuming an injured tone which, even despite the black turmoil of his own thoughts, caused Rob to smile.

Rob allowed Woody to hold his hand in silence. They were all shocked by Kate's sudden death. Apart from Rob, none of them had experienced death at first hand when it involved a generation closer than that of their grandparents. They sat in subdued sympathy, both for the dead girl and for their friend, Rob. Jess and Eddie looked faintly comic, finding themselves sharing an upright chair, Eddie's self-conscious sense of his manhood insisting that the much longer Jess should sit on his lap. Her shoulder pressed against the side of his face; she steadied herself by putting her arm round his neck; his little legs disappeared under her long thighs. Every so often, she needed to balance herself more comfortably by sitting up a little more, tightening her embrace, resulting in Eddie's handsome face being locked in an inescapable cuddle against her shoulder and her bosom, her arm folded under his stubbly chin.

'You look tidier than usual, Woody,' Rob said, studying his friend's clean, neatly pressed trousers, as he tried to respond to their kind attempts at embarrassed normality.

Ever vague about such matters, Woody glanced down and then gave a little gasp.

'Oh, yes! Kate ironed them after washing them.' He paused momentarily. 'It must have been one of the last things she did before…….Oh Rob! I'm sorry…..'

He squeezed Rob's hand hard, fighting back uncharacteristic tears.

Rob choked too and lay back and sighed.

After they had gone, Rob's mind raced round and round like a car competing in the Grand Prix. It was his fault. If Kate and he hadn't struggled, it wouldn't have happened. He now thought of Mara Braithwaite. Oh God! She mustn't know that they had had that awful row. The only other person who had any real knowledge of it was Woody and he had not even met Kate's mother. He might entrust his worry and the truth behind it to Woody. But again, perhaps not. It would upset Woody badly too, especially in the light of his involvement in the quarrel which had hung over those last three days. Also, if he, Rob, decided to keep quiet about the contention on the river bank, having confided in Woody, this might place his friend in an awkward moral position and that would certainly not be fair.

With these tormenting thoughts eddying round like the fierce currents in that terrible river, the double dose of sedatives took hold and Rob entered a fitful and troubled sleep.

SEVEN

Rob was discharged from hospital the next day and, bemused and apprehensive, found himself hailed as a hero. There had been the briefest preliminary call on Mara. She had clung onto him hard but, feeling distraught himself and noticing the presence of Kate's uncle and aunt in the background, he had extricated himself, promising the necessary return visit very soon. He could scarcely bear it when she repeatedly and tearfully thanked him for 'risking his own life in trying to save my precious daughter.' As he left the neat little front garden, he thought of her having lost both her husband and her only daughter almost within a year.

His former school friends at the university gathered round him. His tutors expressed their sympathy and their admiration. Jess and Eddie were especially magnificent. Rob truly appreciated their simple, ham-fisted support, tinged as it regularly was by unintended maladroit humour. They alone did not keep asking him questions. Those questions from others were excruciatingly difficult, partly because the very act of imagination required to live through those dreadful moments again was agony and partly because he could not bear to tell any-one about the ill-tempered struggle which had precipitated the disaster.

It was comforting to sit in Jess's room with Eddie constantly producing mugs of tea and chocolate bars and going on and on and on about his rugby until Jess told him to shut up and biffed him with a cushion. This seemed to be the first move in a well rehearsed game which developed into their having a little scrap on the bed. This always ended up with Eddie's machismo being reduced to squawks and yelps of undignified protest as Jess, entwining him in her long limbs, set about tickling his ribs.

'Geroff me, Woman! What d'you fink yer doin'?'

Then a loud, urgent command, 'No!', followed by a shriek and convulsive laughter when the tough little fitness enthusiast, always dressed in shorts and t-shirt, squirmed and wriggled as, now sprawled horizontally on the bed, he succumbed to his girlfriend's coolly applied, merciless torture. When she paused, he grinned and pronounced the fiction,

'I jus' _let_ 'er win, Rob! Anyfink to keep da wimmin 'appy! NO! STOP!'

Once again he subsided into helpless laughter as Jess, having released him, suddenly pinned down one of his naked shins and proceeded to tickle the sole of his neat small foot. His athletic frame thrashed about on the bed unable to break free. Between the screams and the laughter of agony, Eddie tried to issue stentorian commands but the ritual only ended when Jess again let him go, concluding the episode by briefly lying on top of his exhausted frame and administering a powerful kiss to his moustachioed lips.

Rob even enjoyed the banter which characterised the repetitive and circular arguments which he had with Eddie over the respective merits of the different football teams which they supported. Although she knew nothing about either, Jess always took Rob's side, enjoying the look of disingenuously scandalised amazement which Eddie put on in response to such ignorant and inappropriate intervention.

Rob appreciated their allowing him to share these times of their personal intimacy, recognising it as true, generous, spontaneous friendship.

But these were isolated moments of youthful escape for Rob.

Even as he had stepped out of the hospital, in the company of Woody, Jess and Eddie, a reporter from the Manchester Evening News had been waiting. Eddie had urged Rob to give the interview there and then.

'Mate!' Eddie had informed the reporter. 'Dis guy's a fuckin' hero!'

Jess and Woody had managed to pull Eddie aside while Rob spoke to the reporter. A man with a camera had appeared. When the photograph was published on the front page that evening, the bandage on Rob's arm could be seen. All over the conurbation, people had read about the heroic young student who had 'battled with nature in all its fury in a doomed attempt to rescue the girl he loved.' The headline could be seen on buses, trains and trams, in stations, on news-stands, on the top of high piles in shops, held between the hands of residents in homes from Ashton-under-Lyne to Altrincham, from raw housing estates on the edge of Bolton to plush mansions in Bowden, from red-brick terraced houses in Salford to flats in Stockport:-

'BRAVE ROB'S MERCY DIVE FOR DROWNING GIRL'.

No sooner had he finished with the newspaper reporter than he had been confronted by a woman with a microphone from 'Look Northwest', the regional television news programme and another cameraman. He had tried to explain what had happened in much the same way as he had done to P.C. Hamer. On this occasion he had been more coherent and had succeeded in keeping control of his feelings.

When the programme had been transmitted across the region that evening, Rob had watched it with his three friends. They had all realised that it was hard for him. Woody had been silent. When they had shown the spot by the Mersey where the accident had happened, Jess had not been able to restrain a few tears and had said,

'It's incredible to think she's just……..gone.'

Rob had given a sharp intake of breath. Eddie, sitting between them, had gripped Jess's wrist with his right hand and had placed his left hand firmly on Rob's shoulder.

Then had come the interview with Rob.

'Well — it was just instinctive! I couldn't believe what had happened! I just stripped off and dived in - but it was no good.'

He had lowered his head from the camera but had maintained his composure.

Mothers all over Manchester had said in isolated chorus,

'Oh! That poor boy! What he must be going through!'

Their teenage daughters had noted that Rob was a very sexy guy but, instead of observing the fact, they had harmonised with the sentiments of their mothers.

The press had approached Mara Braithwaite but had the edge of their quest for sensation badly blunted when they were met by Uncle Norman instead who, immediately demolishing any hoped for dramatic effect, kept them on the doorstep and told them in expressionless tone that Kate had been a lovely girl, very talented, with a bright future and that her tragic death would leave a great hole in the lives of her family. He then advised them that they now requested to be left in peace and shut the door.

Rob felt that he ought to obey the summons to London now made by his father. As he set off from Manchester's Piccadilly Station, the world appeared unreal. As the Virgin express slipped down the West Coast main line, it seemed wrong to Rob that all these strangers sharing the carriage were quietly alive whereas Kate was dead. There was a dull, stubborn familiarity about the journey: the dreary urban loftiness of the Stockport viaduct, the huge car scrap-yard as the train approached Stoke-on-Trent, the featureless monotony of the Midlands, scarred by here a cooling tower and there a rash of modern houses erupting on the countryside like acne, the glass and concrete of Milton Keynes as the remaining seats were filled up by preoccupied commuters, the vast, anonymous shopping centre at Watford, seen at an angle as the train swept round a high curve, and then, suddenly, the elliptical arch of Wembley Stadium, the warren of sidings at Stonebridge, and, finally, as the train sank into the last cutting, a row of tall Edwardian terraced villas, once comfortably bourgeois but now flatted out and falling slowly into decay, the grim high-rise flats of Camden Town and the cavernous subterranean gloom of Euston station.

Rob, a Londoner himself, was accustomed to the trudging numbness requisite upon joining the constantly moving, insect immensity of the crowd heaving through the vast complexity of warrens below the metropolis. He followed the wide, stark, tiled passages connecting the main line station with the Underground. He went down, and, again, further down, a sequence of escalators to the Victoria line and boarded a southbound train. The peaceful journey had allowed his sense of shock to merge into a more gentle melancholia and this was cocooned by the blank impersonality of the ever changing city crowd around him. As he emerged to the surface at Pimlico station, finding his own space on a sunlit pavement, fanned by a faint breeze from the Thames, the routine walk home seemed wrongly familiar. Everything looked the same but, of course, it wasn't so. Kate was dead and, suddenly, irrationally, with a renewed force assailing him from the not too distant past, he realised anew, so was his mother. As he waited for the lines of snarling traffic to stop on Vauxhall Bridge Road, the pain associated with her loss stabbed him afresh. If only she could have been here for him now. His father had dutifully asked him back but Rob knew that, however honourable his father's intentions might be, it was unimaginable that he would be able to make any emotional connection with his son in this present situation. Like Kate, Rob was an only child. Gregarious by nature, and inheriting his late mother's looks, personality and social confidence, he had compensated for the lack of siblings by securing strong friendships at school and university. Now, while understanding the well meaning intentions of his father, he dreaded the two days ahead. It would be a difficult week-end.

As he walked along Vauxhall Bridge Road, wrapped in this shroud of sad contemplation, past the tatty ethnic cafes and newsagents, he suddenly noticed a tall black young woman walking in front of him. She was very tall, taller than Rob, and he stood at just under six feet. He checked to see if she was wearing high heels and discovered that her patent leather black shoes were not artificially raised. She was dressed in a closely fitting black suit with sleeves down to her elbows. Rob thought that this enhanced the beauty of her ebony skin. Her black hair was permed into a uniform curl just above her unexpectedly broad shoulders. Her long legs were perfectly shaped, clad in black stockings, the skirt of her suit tapering downwards the length of her thighs, her firm, neat buttocks swaying a little as she walked. Her jacket stopped at her waist, revealing the curves of her hips. From the rear, in temporary fascination, Rob admired her perfectly formed torso, her tailored jacket exactly following the contours of her body. She moved with a lithe grace which animated her wonderful figure. Rob suddenly felt aroused.

As they approached Vauxhall Bridge, the woman continued ahead towards Millbank whereas Rob turned left along John Islip Street. Just as quickly as it had captured him, the spell was broken. Suddenly, he felt ashamed. How could he have been distracted in this particular way when the focus of his thoughts should be Kate's death? Soon he turned into the quiet street of smart terraced townhouses which had been his home all his life. He found his key and began to weep as he turned it in the lock of the empty house, wishing with all his heart that his mother could have been there to embrace him.

A few hours later, Rob was sitting in Oriel's restaurant in Sloane Square facing his father. Suddenly, he realised that, obvious though the fact was, he had never seen his father smiling since his mother's death. In fact, he could not remember him smiling very much even before that dreadful event. Neither, Rob considered, had he ever seen his father shedding tears.

Brian Hadfield, a public school boy of the previous generation, was certainly not incapable of deep feelings but he was quite unable to express these in front of anyone else. After the death of his wife, there were whole nights when he had in fact wept alone. Sometimes, he had given up and dressed at five o'clock in the morning and walked along Millbank as far as Westminster and back, alone amongst night workers coming off shifts and, on the way back, the keenest of the early morning joggers. Now, he inhabited an apparently endless icy depression. His work as an investment banker provided some distraction but little relief. Exact to the point of being pedantic and taking responsibility with uncompromising seriousness, he worried daily about the way his bank, started by his great grandfather but long since taken over by ever larger conglomerates, was conducting its affairs. He believed that he gave cautious, responsible advice to clients but his voice on the board was increasingly ignored. Huge loans were being granted in the belief that they would be returned with interest as the global economy expanded. Men and, more recently, women, half his age, thought his caution quaintly old-fashioned. In recent years, all their masters operated from Wall Street and they hardly bothered to listen to him at all. The euphemism 'sub prime' was just coming into parlance but, as Brian Hadfield's younger colleagues sat in the wine bars in the City, they laughed about it as a distant joke played out in Florida by a few provincial redneck hicks. His salary was high; commissions were good; he managed his own investments carefully; he was still surprised by the bonus some computer in New York awarded him and felt increasingly affronted by a loud, foul mouthed arriviste with an East End accent who complained about not getting enough. How colleagues had changed since he had started after leaving school nearly forty years ago. What would his great-grandfather, Robert, have made of it all, the man who had steered his own bank though the Great Depression of the 1870s? Or his grandfather, also Robert, who had helped the institution to survive the Wall Street crash of 1929? He had written and published, at his own expense, a history of the bank since its foundation a hundred-and-fifty years ago but no-one seemed much interested.

How sad he looks, thought Rob miserably. He had an impulsive desire to reach across the table and touch his father, or get up and hug him but any such action was, of course, totally out of the question. His father would have been furious, embarrassed and upset. The presence of the table between them, with the paraphernalia of cutlery, glasses and napkins, seemed emblematic. As his father was gloomily perusing the wine list, it occurred to Rob that perhaps he had himself inherited his father's apparent capacity to shut off emotionally challenging situations, despite his, Rob's, greater ability to relate to other people. He thought again about the issue with Kate and how he had, with cold decision, closed the book on the matter the next day and proceeded with the rest of his life with measured determination. Although he had felt so much closer to his mother, he was also his father's son.

The waiter came. They made their choices and Brian Hadfield selected an appropriate bottle of wine and requested a jug of tap-water. Relieved of the burden of the bulky menus, father and son faced each other directly across the table. Brian Hadfield's watery blue eyes looked directly into the expressive dark eyes of his son; he recognised his wife's eyes.

'So, Rob, when is the funeral?'

'Friday. They just fixed it before I left.'

'Do you know the time?'

'Two o'clock, I think. I'll have to check,'

'I'll be there with you, Son.'

And, rather unnecessarily, as if to disengage from the risk of a moment's public intimacy, Brian Hadfield took his diary out of his breast pocket and entered a note with the fine tip of a small gold ball-point pen.

Rob's immediate surprise was quickly mitigated by a sense of gratitude for the gesture. After all, Dad was all he really had and, yes, it was important to him, he realised, that his father should be there for him. Now he longed to share the messy truth about those dreadful moments on the river bank but, instinctively, he knew that that would be one disclosure too far.

'How are you coping, Son?'

'Oh —all-right, I suppose. I mean, it's been an awful shock.'

It sounded such a trite statement of the obvious.

His father nodded.

Rob waited but, realising that his father did not know what to say next, he felt impelled to break the silence himself.

'It's been a bit grim really, hasn't it? First Mum and now this.'

His father dropped his eyes and Rob realised that his platitudes were doing more harm than good. Why, he wondered, had he been so stupid as to bring that up? He knew that his father never wanted to talk about it. And to introduce it at a moment like this: Oh dear!

The weekend continued in the same vein and Rob felt relieved on the Sunday afternoon when the train pulled out of Euston and, leaving the spire of Harrow Church behind, swept him forward into the sunlit countryside of Hertfordshire. There had been so much in the house to remind him of his mother. Nothing had been moved. His own bedroom remained the same. It had been a place of childhood joy. His children's books were still on the shelves, unused for years now, not even gathering dust. An outdated Manchester United poster was still attached to the wall, depicting a youthful David Beckham before he left the team. When Rob had lovingly measured the Blu-Tack with which to stick it up, he had no idea that he would be attending university at the shrine of his hero, albeit by then departed. His carefully selected collection of toy soldiers stood sentinel on the mantel-piece, a childhood craze which had passed with adolescence, a chapter from what seemed to Rob long ago, yet still haunting in its precise definition. Now it all seemed to be the innocent happiness of an irrecoverable past. Not for the first time he wished that he had brothers and sisters, like most of his friends.

As the train passed Berkhamsted Castle, scene of ancient strife, he set about texting his friends in Manchester to tell them of his return. Almost immediately, he received a return message from Eddie. For the first time that weekend, Rob's face broke into its natural smile, his mother's smile, as his father had so often painfully and silently observed.

EIGHT

He had visited Mara the next afternoon after concluding his academic commitments. It had been predictably difficult, especially as she had persisted in expressing the depth of her gratitude to him for his attempt to save her daughter. It had been impossible to tell her that they had had such an appalling row immediately before Kate's death.

When he returned to the flat, only Woody was in. His friend was in the sitting room, idly watching a children's nature programme on the television. Woody pressed the mute on the remote when Rob came into the room. His shoeless feet rested on the coffee table. He was slumped on the old sofa. An empty coffee mug shared the table with his feet.

'Hi Mate! How did you get on in London with your Dad?'

'Thanks for asking, Mate. It was difficult. He did his best, I suppose. We went out for a meal on Saturday and then again for lunch yesterday. He's coming up for the funeral on Friday. It's decent of him really. But, the fact is, we just can't seem to talk to each other about it. It was the same when my Mum died. He just shuts up like a clam and looks miserable. He's always been a bit like that but it's got a lot worse since Mum went.'

Rob crashed onto the sofa beside Woody.

'Well, I guess that that's your Dad. But how are *you*, Mate?'

Rob hesitated. But then, Hell, he'd kept his feelings from his father and, with enormous effort, he had tried not to collapse on Mara Braithwaite (though he had shed some tears). He *had to* find a shoulder to weep on somewhere. Jess and Eddie were great but, somehow, he couldn't really enter emotional territory with them. Somehow, too, despite their kindness in including him in their lives, he sensed that they wouldn't want this either. They wouldn't cope. There would be the constant unspoken given that they were a happily fulfilled item together whereas Rob's relationship had ended in disaster. Woody had asked the question and so he decided to give a straight answer.

'Well, Mate. If you really want to know, I feel bloody awful!'

Woody didn't suddenly rise up with a gush of sympathy nor did he recoil as one placed precipitately out of his depth. Beyond flicking the television off altogether, he didn't move. He kept his eyes intently on his friend, knowing that it was for Rob to talk as much or as little as he pleased.

'I can't believe that this has all happened: that she's dead and that we had that stupid row and that…. well….it's all my fault.'

'It's not your fault if there was an accident on the river bank.'

'No, I guess not.'

'It wasn't your fault about the row. If it was anybody's, it was mine. First, I made such a mess in the kitchen and then ….well…. you were right to be mad with me when you came into Kate's room. You know, Mate, there *was* nothing between us. I just felt guilty about having caused all the trouble and she was so upset that she just needed some-one to hug her and….er….well…. I was just there. I know what it must have looked like but I can only promise you that there was nothing in it: at least, nothing beyond a bit of compassion and sympathy, all mixed up with me feeling guilty about having started it all.'

'Yeah Mate, I accept that. I was jumping to conclusions. She was mad at me and then I was mad at her and…. Oh God! If only it hadn't happened, we could all have been OK now, instead of having to go through this. And poor Katie: she's been *killed!* I've just come from her mother; I could hardly stand it. And, Woody, it's like I didn't trust you either, when you've been such a good mate. That was wrong too. In fact, I seem to have got everything wrong!'

Rob's dark eyes moistened but he kept back the sobs which were bursting to emerge.

'You mustn't torture yourself like this. There was an ordinary row, the sort of row I guess students sharing flats must have all the time. And then there was a terrible accident, an accident that was nobody's fault, unless we're going to blame the rain, or the river. What's happened *is* terrible but, Mate, you're not responsible for blind forces: the weather, the river, the slippery towpath, Kate slipping. You can't take the blame for the causal factors in a situation like this. You're only a bloke; you're not God!'

As he looked at Rob, Woody's eyes softened into a smile. Having delivered his peroration on metaphysical morality, he scratched an itch on his stomach and crossed one foot over the other on the coffee table. He gently rubbed the toe of his left foot under his right shin; he was an itchy sort of guy.

Rob moved closer to Woody on the sofa.

'Thanks Mate. What you say is true. You're a real friend. I'm very lucky to have you as a friend.'

A lot of Rob felt profound gratitude to his friend. He was about to hug Woody but then stopped and, instead, he put his head in his hands.

Woody now put his feet on the floor and sat up straighter.

'What is it Rob?'

'Oh! It *is* all my fault! It's *my fucking fault!*'

Woody felt that friendship alone compelled him now to ask the question which had been privately gestating in his mind ever since the event.

'Mate, tell me to mind my own business if you like and, of course, you only need to answer this if you think it would help, but, when you and she met on the tow-path, did anything happen, or what?'

'There was a struggle. She tried to stop me getting past her. I didn't want to speak to her. I was still angry with her.'

He paused.

'No need to answer this, Mate, but do you think she'd have fallen in if there hadn't been a struggle?

'I don't know.'

But he did.

At that moment, the door bell for the flat rang. This was such an unusual occurrence that Rob, already on edge, jumped off the sofa.

'I'll get it,' said Woody.

A few moments later he showed in P.C. Hamer.

Woody made a discreet withdrawal.

'I'll be in the kitchen, Rob. By the way, I'm cooking for us this evening.'

P.C. Hamer sat down in the armchair to the right of Rob.

'You seem to have a good pal there, Rob.'

'I certainly have. He's been my rock through this.'

'What about your parents?'

'Mum's dead. Dad's in London.'

There was a brief awkward pause. Stuart Hamer was a sensitive young man and didn't want to press it any further.

'Well, Rob, I'm sorry to intrude Mate, but, as I explained in the hospital, I just need to secure your statement. It's just a formality, really, but I'm sure that you'll understand that when a fatal accident has occurred we need a formal statement. That's all.'

Rob acquiesced.

The policeman read the original statement out and asked Rob if there was anything he wanted to change.

Rob said that there wasn't.

'So, you both met on the tow-path and embraced. Kate then lost her footing on the slippery path and fell into the river. You stripped off and jumped in to try to save her.'

Now Rob did start to sob.

'Rob, I'm really sorry. I apologise for having to come here and drag you through it all again so soon. If you agree with what has been written, all you need to do is to sign it and then I'll clear off and leave you alone. It looks as though you've got a good friend here to help you out.'

'No, I'm sorry to be like this. You've been very kind. It's just all been so awful.'

'I understand. God, I know what I'd feel like if it were me.'

Stuart waited for Rob to recover. Then the document was signed and the constable got up to take his leave. They shook hands at the front door. Rob went back to the kitchen and accepted the beer and crisps which Woody offered him.

In due course, the coroner's verdict was to record accidental death.

The funeral was predictably grim. Kate was buried beside her father. There had been some difficulty about this but Norman and Jane were acquainted with the local vicar and he had intervened on the family's behalf. Mara, in the madness of her sudden grief, had been very awkward to deal with. She had refused to have a service in any church and so, as had been the case for Harry, there was a short committal at the graveside. Manchester chose to go into characteristic mourning for the occasion. It was a day of relentless gloom and the rain started at lunch-time. The vicar's white cassock was ruffled by the damp westerly wind. Umbrellas were effective only to the degree that they kept people's heads dry. Rob sheltered under his father's umbrella. Woody, Jess and Eddie were fully exposed to the rain, as were a couple of Rob's former school friends who had decently turned up to support him, dressed in their old public school charcoal grey suits. A cluster of Kate's school friends had travelled back from various universities and huddled under flimsy, brightly coloured umbrellas, shocked and tearful and wearing skirts which gave no protection below their thighs and heels which sank into the mud. Two ladies from the Citizens' Advice Bureau stood discreetly under umbrellas. The neighbours came and one, a retired civil servant, helped to fit the young people into cars and assisted Brian Hadfield to call a taxi for Rob and himself and Rob's two old school chums.

They all went back to the semi-detached house in Cheadle Hulme where Jane and Norman took charge. Jane had organised it all. Tea was served, together with sandwiches and cakes. Several people accepted a glass of Amontillado sherry from Norman in an attempt to recover from the chill dampness to which they had so recently been exposed. Ironically, the awkwardness of the crush in the small rooms helped to break the ice. Everyone did their best. Curiously, Brian Hadfield probably found it easier than anyone else. The occasion rather suited a solemn man who lived a solemn life. Mara, Jane and Norman found him absolutely gracious. ('You would expect no less from Rob's father, of course: so good of him to leave his work and come all the way from London. And it wasn't as though he had been without his own sorrows either.') He said all the right things and, to be fair, he meant them. He had a sustained conversation with Norman and the civil servant neighbour, Cyril Banks, and the three gentlemen found that they were much in accord over the state of the country. The Prime Minister's ears should have been burning.

Mara was unbelievably brave throughout. She was clearly very pleased to see all the young people there, Kate's friends, and deeply touched that some of Rob's friends came as well. Only, right at the end, when they were leaving, and she was saying good-bye to Rob, did she suddenly, though momentarily, break down. Rob felt terribly sorry for her but he just couldn't hug her in front of all these people and he had his own confused feelings too. However, Jane stepped in promptly and Brian Hadfield put his arm through that of his son and ushered him gently away.

NINE

It was the second Monday in November.

Years back, Manchester had been justifiably angry when its weather had been cited as one of the reasons for its not being awarded the Olympic Games for the Millennium. Sydney, the over-triumphant victors, pressed home the image of sun-tanned Ozzies sprawled *en masse* on Bondi Beach, the Harbour Bridge and the Opera House impressively complementing the blue waters of its immense harbour. People outside the city laughed when Manchester claimed that its annual rainfall was less than that of Sydney. The Mancunians were accurate in their claim. However, the trouble is that, whereas Sydney is prey to ferocious, sudden downpours, in Manchester, for long periods, although it might not actually be raining, it can seem constantly threatening to do so and, when it does rain, although the precipitation may not always be heavy, the dampness can hang about in the city's great bowl under the Pennine massif to the east which shelters its sunnier Yorkshire rivals. This climate was, of course, the key to Manchester's immense prosperity in the past, the dampness suiting the manufacture of the cotton brought in conveniently from the west as the ships plied between Savannah, Georgia, and Liverpool, their precious cargo then transported up the Ship Canal.

For several days now, a grey pall had hung over the conurbation. The drizzle was so fine that people were not always certain whether it was there or not. They felt its penetrating chill as they wrapped up in fleeces and water-proofs. The coughs and colds of the winter were beginning. The exhaust fumes from the congested traffic could not escape into the atmosphere. A slimy patina stuck to the pavements. Lights stayed on all day. The last chrysanthemums withered on their stalks in suburban gardens. Eddie wore a green fleece on top of his shorts as he took his afternoon run round Platt Fields. Flecks of mud sprayed onto his white socks and his shins.

Rob had been putting off his next visit to Mara Braithwaite and, guiltily, he had not responded to her calls left on his mobile. When he had seen her number coming up on the previous evening, however, he felt at last compelled to respond and now, following his afternoon seminar, he was sitting on top of the 45 as it ground through Rusholme, looking down on the halal shops, the green-grocers with their vegetables in stalls outside, small hardware stores with redbrick flats over the shop, queues of assorted people waiting to board the bus: Moslem women in burqas, students in frayed jeans, trainers and, oblivious to the weather, short-sleeved t-shirts, workmen with canvas bags slung over their shoulders, old ladies dressed in macs carrying small shopping bags, giggling girls travelling home from work together. Slowly the bus inched forwards, the whine of the engine agitating against the restraint of the automatic clutch. A guy on a bike cut past on the inside, braking sharply when a delivery van suddenly moved off from the kerb, the bike's brakes issuing a diminishing howl of protest. Further on, at Old Hall Lane, the bus filled up with uniformed boys from the Manchester Grammar School and girls from the High School: a cheerful, noisy, laughing crowd, chaffing each other, joking about some embarrassment in a lesson with old so-and-so who had missed some point, planning a Saturday night out together, texting like mad, apparently without a care in the world, oblivious to the world around them.

Rob felt terribly alone with his problem and it wouldn't go away. He didn't feel that he could take it any further, not even with Woody. Woody, after all, must *know* the truth - he was a shrewd chap - but he had been too decent and too wise to raise the issue again. The secret was safe with him. His loyalty was guaranteed and, in any case, no specific admission had been made even to him. So far as every-one else was concerned, the matter was closed. Kate had gone out to meet her boyfriend on the tow-path of the Mersey; they had embraced; the path was slippery; she had slipped and fallen in; he had done everything humanly possible to rescue her but it was impossible to do so and Kate had tragically drowned. Nobody's fault at all: death by misadventure. It was totally convincing and there it could be left.

And, of course, it was partly true; certainly, the end of the story was accurate; and, of course, Rob hadn't intended the accident to happen, let alone its terrible consequence; and, yes, it *was* an accident. But….but….

Now, he was again balancing the Spode cup on its saucer. On what now seemed a long distant previous visit, he had remarked on the beauty of the china. He had been mildly embarrassed when Mara had quietly and bravely mentioned that it had been a wedding present.

'It's good of you to come, Rob. You mustn't feel under any obligation, really. You've got your own life ahead of you and you must pick up the pieces and move on. '

'Mrs Braithwaite —Mara —I can't imagine how awful it must be for *you*.'

'Well, yes, I can't deny it. It might have been easier if Harry had still been alive.'

Rob sat quietly and put the tea-cup down.

'You were the last person to see Katie alive, Rob, and you were embracing each other when it happened. There's something lovely about that at least.'

He could stand it no longer. He had come with the intention of somehow telling her the full story but had, so far, been stalling. Now he blurted it out.

'It wasn't quite like that, Mara. I hadn't wanted to tell you but I feel I shouldn't conceal the truth. Kate and I had had a quarrel two days before it happened.'

'Oh, I'm sorry to hear that. What about? Or perhaps you'd rather not say?'

'It was something about nothing really- which somehow makes it worse. It happened just after we had been round here for Sunday lunch. Our flat-mate, Woody —I think you met him at the funeral- had left the kitchen in a mess. Kate complained to him. I felt that she was over-reacting. She then accused me of taking Woody's side. And — well —it went on from there. We weren't speaking.'

'It sounds pretty normal to me. Young people sharing a place together are likely to get on each other's nerves occasionally. So what was happening at the river when you were embracing? Were you making it up?'

She gave a little smile of rueful indulgence.

'No. We weren't embracing. Kate followed me out when I went for my run. She approached the spot from the opposite direction. When we met, the dispute continued. Or, to be frank she wanted to make up but I didn't. She tried to stop me running on. There was a struggle. She slipped and fell in. I jumped in after her but the current was too strong. I couldn't save her.'

Mara Braithwaite sat motionlessly, her eyes widening as she tried to absorb the horror of the words which she had just heard.

'You mean —you pushed her in!'

'No! I didn't push her in! Like I said, there was a struggle. She slipped. I couldn't save her in time.'

In his agitation, he flushed with sudden anger. This was awful enough without her misinterpreting it to make it even worse. God knows, He was *not* guilty of murder!

'Don't you raise your voice at me after what you've just admitted!'

He was, with equal suddenness, abashed and alarmed.

'I —I'm sorry. That was out of order.'

"Out of order' you call it! 'Out of order'! When you have just told me that you have pushed my daughter into the Mersey, where she drowned!'

'I DIDN'T PUSH HER! SHE FELL AS WE WERE HAVING A STRUGGLE! She tried to prevent me from passing.'

It was intolerable that she should magnify the horror, locked into this accusatory invention.

'You're a big strong lad. She was only a little girl!'

'Oh God! I've told you! I can't do anything more! I'd do *anything* to turn the clock back. It was an *accident!* Don't think that I'm enjoying this any more than anyone else.'

She sat now, looking at the immaculately vacuumed patterned carpet, her hands folded. She rocked just slightly to and fro.

'You killed my daughter. If it wasn't for you, she'd still be alive.'

Rob had known that the disclosure would be far from easy but he had not quite anticipated *this*. He wanted to go but felt he shouldn't. He couldn't leave her at this juncture. Also, there was a real need now to put the record straight. It was quite bad enough without this woman making it much worse.

'It's murder. That's what it is. You've *murdered* her. Oh, MY GOD!'

She was now shrieking hysterically and tears started to gush from her eyes.

Rob got up and attempted to embrace her but she rose from her chair.

'Don't you touch me! Don't you dare come near me! You despicable wretch! You've killed my daughter! You SWINE!'

Though increased in volume, her voice went bizarrely low in gradually comprehending rage.

'Get out of my house! I'm going straight to the police with this! I'm going to see you locked up in Strangeways Gaol for the rest of your days!'

Rob was himself now weeping aloud in shock and terror.

He fled from the house.

He had to share all this with some-one. Woody was the only person conceivable.

This time, he didn't restrain his tears as the story tumbled out. Woody sat impassively. He guessed that Rob could do with a hug but he, Woody, wasn't really into hugging other blokes and so he felt that it was best to recognise this limitation and then to try to pick up some of the pieces when his friend's emotional narrative finally concluded.

'Oh, Woody, what the fuck am I to do?'

'Right, Mate. I don't want to sound cold and hard but we've got loads of feelings sloshing about here —quite understandably —and I reckon that these need to be put into place by some cold rational thought. Does that seem fair?'

'Yeah, Mate! That's why I've fucking come to you! I don't know what the fuck to do!'

'Well, I'm not going to say I'm right but let's just look at this coldly. Disagree if you want to. It wasn't murder, for God's sake — you know that yourself —and neither was it manslaughter. It was an accident, as I said before. I didn't know all this latest but I'd guessed that something like it had happened.

'Yeah, I thought you had. You're quite bright, I know.'

'Thanks for the patronising.'

'Oh no! Sorry Mate! You're my best friend. I didn't mean to be *patronising!* Oh God! I can't seem to do anything right! I hadn't even told *you* all this!'

'Enough dramatising! I'd guessed it! Anyway, to the point! It was dreadful that Kate slipped fatally but that was not your responsibility. The verdict declared 'accidental death' and that is just what it was. All-right, there was a struggle but you didn't push her in; you didn't ask her to fall in! You didn't ask her to try to stop you passing on the tow-path. In so far as there's any responsibility, it was hers. I myself am really sorry that Kate drowned —it is horrible —but you are NOT to let yourself assume false blame for it. Anyway, Rob —come on, you need to use your brain in this, not just your heart —there is no *evidence* to back up her mother's false allegation, made, understandably, when she was in a state of hysterical distress. There were no witnesses. No-one can disprove your account of the incident (which is, of course, the true one). No policeman or magistrate will want to go into a theoretical alternative from someone who wasn't even there, who, in any case, has an emotionally charged vested interest. I know this sounds hard but it is really important that you don't destroy yourself over a nasty fiction which a tragically bereaved mother is trying to torture you with. *You didn't push her in. She fell. Accidental death. Finish. Right?*'

This time, Woody's words did penetrate Rob's brain and they even touched his soul with a preliminary sense of rest.

TEN

Mara Braithwaite sat still for a long time after Rob's departure. She wanted to get up and run round the house shrieking and smashing things. But her innate self-control and common sense did not completely desert her even in such extremis. What good after all would that do? How would it alter anything? Instead, she sat still and wept until the tears blinded her and her handkerchief was saturated. She felt devastated and utterly alone. There was, however, one thing to hold onto and it became ever clearer and firmer as the hours ticked silently by. Reparation had to be made for the capital wrong done to her daughter. She had never considered the concept of revenge before, let alone understood it or experienced it. Now, she knew, with the satisfaction of total certainty, that her implacable and undeviating mission in life was to bring to justice and to destroy that boy, that whited sepulchre, that angel of destruction. She took some solace in the thought of his father suffering in the future something of what she herself was enduring now.

A cup of tea provided some mild restorative. She pulled a cardigan around her shoulders, tidied the kitchen and sat down again. How could she secure her end, her righteous end?

The police must be told. The boy had lied to them. Or, at the very least, he had withheld vital information, germane to the truth, the even more hideous truth, at the centre of that final encounter. The problem was, she realised early on, that he would lie to them again. He would even deny the admission which he had made to her. With cold fury, she could visualise the circumstance when some young policewoman would sit her down and explain to her, as if she were speaking to a child or an idiot, that the allegation made was not substantiated by any evidence. There were after all no witnesses to either the assault or her last conversation with Rob. Criminals got away with anything these days, murder included. You only needed to read the papers or switch on the television news to understand that. But she, Mara Braithwaite, Katie's mother, would be revenged - within or without the law. If she ended up being sent to prison too, because the law could not or would not discharge its responsibilities, what did she care? She had nothing to lose now. Her destiny was the execution of this one great task. She would destroy that boy.

For the next few days she thought of nothing else. She kept herself going by living in a world of violent fantasy.

She remembered a poem by William Blake from away back in her school days. She took the book out of the library and read 'A Poison Tree' several times each day. Soon, she found that she had memorised it.

'I was angry with my friend:
I told my wrath, my wrath did end.
I was angry with my foe:
I told it not, my wrath did grow.

And I watered it in fears,
Night and morning with my tears:
And I sunned it with smiles,
And with soft deceitful wiles.

And it grew both day and night,
Till it bore an apple bright.
And my foe beheld it shine,
And he knew that it was mine.

And into my garden stole,
When the night had veiled the pole;
In the morning glad I see,
My foe outstretched beneath the tree'

Yes, she could wait. There was something satisfying in this waiting. She might not yet have devised an effective plan but she could feel her own poison tree growing inside her, as she had felt dear Katie doing so all those years ago, and, while she waited, she would water it night and morning.

As she walked along the High Street and watched a bus going past, she took delight in imagining Rob slipping from the kerb, in much the same way as Katie must have done from the tow-path, and falling under its wheels. *'The wheels of the bus go round and round'* Harry had used to sing to Katie. Yes, well let them *'go round and round'* again, now, crushing the body of that hateful boy. A workman was piercing the surface of the road with a pneumatic drill. The terrible noise was good, the more so as she imagined Rob's handsome face directly on the receiving end of the drill, being savagely and painfully destroyed. She stood on the footbridge above the railway and imagined Rob tied to the lines. She waited for a train to pull out of the suburban station and pretended that it was accelerating over a screaming Rob, fully but helplessly aware of his dreadful fate, a blind mechanical force cutting through his shins and his neck, decapitating him. She nursed these fantasies as she went to bed at night and, after a fitful sleep, she added to them daily. She had never felt remotely like this before but, oh! it was good. It was the only way *to* feel in a cruel and evil world which had nevertheless provided a readily identifiable focus for her just hatred in the person of that diabolical boy.

On one occasion she took the bus up to Didsbury and waited at a distance to catch a glimpse of the object of her intended destruction. By now, bright yellow leaves had fallen from the trees, festooning hedges and shrubs and carpeting the pavement with gold: beauty in death, the paradox of late autumn. Her hour long wait was finally rewarded when Rob emerged from the house alone. He appeared to have acquired or borrowed a bicycle. He stooped to tuck his trousers into his socks, unlocked the bicycle and cycled off towards Wilmslow Road. He did not notice her as she stood motionless behind a tree some fifty metres from the house, wrapped in a hooded dark cagoule. This total lack of awareness of his own impending doom was in itself strangely satisfying. The shock of the moment when it came, in whatever form this was to be, would be a climax of fulfilled ecstasy. She considered returning the next day, armed with a kitchen knife, and running across the road, knocking him off his bike and, as he lay on the road in surprise, falling upon him and stabbing him repeatedly before he could defend himself. But perhaps that was too risky; she might misjudge the moment of attack and, if she missed, they could be reduced to more equal combat when he would be more than capable of disarming her. As a child, she had always opened her Christmas presents carefully and slowly, delaying what she had anticipated to be the finest and most thrilling until the end. The intensely pleasurable prospect of destroying the hated enemy was something to be nurtured for a little time yet. There should be some days at least of imagining a variety of gruesome possibilities.

Back at home, in Katie's room, she found photographs of Rob. There was still one, in a light coloured wooden frame, standing on her daughter's little desk, between a miniature woolly pink elephant and a block of multi-coloured post-it sheets. As she entered the room and looked at it, she almost literally felt her heart breaking, pulled apart between the grieving desolation of bereavement and a surge of furious hatred. As she lifted the picture and looked down at it intently, she also felt incredulity. There was the handsome face, with the smiling dark eyes and the strong bone structure, the clean dark hair, conventionally cut but uncombed, the lovely young man, who had brought so much happiness and hope into their lives, but who was in fact a devil. She released a hoarse, inarticulate cry and brought the picture down with all the force she could command on the corner of the wooden desk. The smashed glass scattered. She extracted the sheet of paper. There was a hole through Rob's neck from which creases now fanned. She crunched the paper up in her right hand. Shards of glass trapped in her palm created stabs of sharp pain and spurts of blood. She didn't care. This is what she would be doing in reality soon, perhaps very soon. She went through the drawers of Katie's desk and quickly found more photographs of him. She selected one in which they were standing together, his arm round her shoulder, hers around his waist. She picked up a pair of scissors from the top of the desk and carefully cut, so far as she could, the line of separation between their two bodies. Having thus detached Rob from Katie, she tore him into tiny shreds and threw him into the waste-paper basket, returning her daughter to the folder whence the photograph came. She also found an excellent picture of Rob on his own, dressed in white tennis shorts and shirt. Yes- what young girl wouldn't fall in love with a boy who looked like that and who took notice of her? That figure, that smile! She found a red ball-point pen and, putting the photograph down flat on the desk, she drew a diagonal cross through Rob, the lines cutting from his shoulders to his thighs, intersecting approximately over his heart. She pressed so hard that the pen tore the paper. Then, she drew another line, vertically downwards, slicing his head in two, crossing his chest, again intersecting the other two strokes over his heart and then incising his crotch and genitals. With her hand still bleeding from the fragments of glass embedded in it, she again crumpled the maimed picture and flung it into the bin behind the others.

She went into the bathroom and spent more than three-quarters of an hour extracting the pieces of glass from her hand and bathing it in iodine. The searing pain was right! Oh- *so* right! It gave physical expression to her inner feelings and it provided a proleptic symbol for the fate awaiting that damnable, bloody boy.

She made excuses about not being able to attend the Citizens' Advice Bureau and, after having done that three times, she withdrew altogether. Rain had set in with the darkening evenings. She sat for hours without moving in the silent house, locked in melancholy reverie.

It was a sudden shock when the phone rang. The clarion call of intrusive normality cut through the private Hell which she had been nurturing so assiduously.

'Mara, love, it's Jane.' The melancholy music of the Manchester vowels suited the speaker's feminine compassion. 'I know that you asked to be left in peace but Norman and I do worry about you and we just want to see how you are.'

'It's kind of you to phone, Jane. I'm all-right: bearing up.'

In a sort of trance, Mara agreed to go over to them for lunch on Sunday. She regretted it as soon as the call had finished. But what did it matter, whether she went or stayed. Out of habit, she wouldn't break an arrangement made. She couldn't bear to phone back and cancel and be maddened by listening to Jane's lengthy protestations.

On the next Sunday, she took the 45 up to the centre of town and then a tram into the north of the city. At the various stops in Didsbury, and Withington, the bus filled with students. They were a gregarious bunch. As it was a Sunday, Mara imagined that they were all going off to disperse into a variety of pleasurable activities once they reached the city centre.

A smiling, bright-eyed lad of about twenty sat next to her, joking with his friends in the seats around. They were off to play football. Aware that Rob was a soccer enthusiast, Mara looked round cautiously and was relieved to see that he was not among them. Despite the cold, the lad next to her was wearing just a white t-shirt and blue jeans. He held a hold-all across his lap. The bus was crowded. When several more young people boarded at Fallowfield, they had to stand in the aisle. The hold-all was edged into Mara's space. Surreptitiously, she tried to push it back.

'I'm really sorry', said the young man politely. 'I've got another guy's kit in here as well as my own. It makes it bulky.'

He turned the bag vertically, holding it between his knees and hugging it uncomfortably in his bare arms, resting his chin on the top. He gave a carefree laugh, inviting complicit understanding.

Mara smiled an acknowledgement but was too shy to say anything. After this briefest of brushes with human reality, she disappeared into her own gloomy inner landscape again. How happy all these young people are, she had thought, full of vitality and good humour, without a care in the world. Her Katie might have been like this too, even now, at this very moment, if she hadn't met that damned boy. In her black reverie, she turned her attention away from her neighbour and the high-spirited youthfulness which surrounded her, and looked out of the window. She hardly heard the merry sounds inside the bus as she looked out into the surly Manchester gloom of early winter. The high railings of All Saints pierced the greyness, the building behind looming Blakean black.

Jane had, predictably, gone to much trouble with the lunch. Mara had to admit that a carefully cooked Sunday roast was a welcome change from the microwave ready meals upon which she had been subsisting for the past month. Norman's small glass of Amontillado sherry was welcome too. Mara had not consumed any alcohol since the disaster had happened. It was easy to let Jane chatter on. Mara gave perfunctory answers which she hoped might stem excessively intrusive enquiries. She even felt rather relaxed in the comfortable armchair after lunch. The carefully sipped glass of wine took effect and, after so many days in the solitude of torturing, introspective tension, she dozed off quite peacefully.

Jane and Norman gave knowing looks to each other and tiptoed around her as they cleared up. It was quite a shock for Mara when she returned to consciousness to find the lights on in response to the gathering darkness outside. Tea and cakes were ready waiting and the best flowery bone china was set out.

When, in some trepidation, duty bound by her faith, Jane gently intimated that Norman and she had been planning to attend the evening service at their nonconformist church and, guessing that Mara's views on Christianity would not have become any less hostile after the recent horror, she very tentatively asked her if she might like to accompany them, offering the carrot that, afterwards, Norman would be happy to drive her home, Mara, unwilling to muster the energy to apply any resistance, agreed.

The United Reform Church was a soiled redbrick affair on a busy main road which it now shared with a fish and chip shop, two Halal food shops, a Pakistani chemist, whose cousin ran the neighbouring newsagent's, a Polish delicatessen, a sad outlet for a local cancer charity and an optimistic estate agent. The vandalised bus shelter outside the church harboured the sodden litter of the weekend. Inside, the building had a mock Gothic vaulted interior. The wood round the interior was painted an unyielding light blue; the ceiling, above dark wooden beams, was a dirty white. The Victorian pews had been replaced by even more uncomfortable plastic chairs.

Jane introduced Mara to Jean, a bespectacled retired librarian and a spinster, dressed in grey tweed, as the latter handed out a copy of 'Mission Praise' and a printed A5 sheet of notices. It was clear to Mara that Jean must have been fully apprised of her situation from the look of knowing sympathy which was bestowed upon her as she pronounced 'welcome' with muted sobriety. Mara thought it likely that Jean had been called up to pray for her, no doubt along with half of the rest of the congregation. She instantly wished that she hadn't come.

Mara was placed on one of the plastic chairs half way along the church, sitting between Jane and Norman. Some youngish people were at the front providing music. A thin man in his thirties, with lank brown hair and heavy glasses, was playing a guitar accompaniment to a slightly younger woman who was singing into a microphone. A youth provided some percussion with a pair of cymbals and a prim looking young woman, also with spectacles, tried to provide a descant with a recorder. On either side of her, Jane and Norman bowed their heads in prayer.

In due course, the volume of the music was lowered reverentially and the woman sang,

'Be still, for the presence of the Lord, the Holy One is here.
Come bow before Him now with reverence and fear.
In Him no sin is found; we stand on Holy ground.
Be still, for the presence of the Lord, the Holy One, is here.'

The musicians took their seats. The pastor, clad in jeans and a woolly jumper, perhaps rather too obviously asserting a genial informality for the benefit of the younger members of the congregation, commenced the service by welcoming any visitors. Mara was momentarily terrified that she might be picked out to stand up, or something equally dreadful but, mercifully, she was spared.

The first hymn was announced and the congregation rose to sing.

'Ascribe greatness to our God, the Rock,
His work is perfect and all His ways are just.'

Mara did not know the hymn or the tune but she did take in the words. She tried hard not to shudder with revulsion at, for her, their palpable untruth. Jane's clear tones rang out beside her. Who are these people, Mara thought? How can she expect to sing about God being 'just' when, if He exists at all (which, frankly, Mara thought extremely unlikely), His justice sees fit to rob her of her husband and her daughter within a year or so? She immediately wanted to get out but, trapped as she was, escape was impossible.

The visiting preacher was welcomed. He was introduced as the vice-principal of a theological college. A grey-haired man, wearing a suit and a clerical collar, ascended into the pulpit. The church had been following a series on The Lord's Prayer and they had come to the section calling for the receiving and giving of forgiveness, where God is asked to:-

'Forgive us our sins as we forgive those who sin against us.'

After the introductory prayer and preamble, Mara, perhaps because of the total absence of any alternative, found herself tuning in to the monologue being delivered in front of her and above her. Pulpits in nonconformist churches are large and elevated. There is no altar; the Word is all important. The reverend doctor spoke clearly in Received Pronunciation.

'Forgiveness is the Clapham Junction of our Faith, or, since I am here in Manchester, should I say the Manchester Victoria? All lines must lead to it.

Let us be frank. There are times when none of us finds it easy to forgive and there may even be situations where it really does seem humanly impossible to forgive. Suppose it was <u>your</u> family wiped out by an air raid in Afghanistan. Suppose it was one of <u>your</u> loved ones killed in the attack on the World Trade Centre on 11 September 2001. Suppose it was <u>your</u> child fatally knocked down by *a speeding drunk driver. An ordained lady in Bristol gave up her ministry because she <u>could not</u> forgive the suicide bomber who murdered her daughter on the London Underground on 7 July 2005.*

It is impossible to stand here and tell such people that they are wrong. In every case, it is surely humanly impossible for these people to forgive. And yet —<u>and yet</u> —in two cases amongst the lamentable spate of fatal stabbings in South London within the last year or so, two mothers, one as it happens black, the other white, separated in their bereavement by months, publicly <u>forgave</u> the youths who murdered their completely innocent sons. In both cases they were Christian women and, I suggest to you, it would have been impossible for them to have found the ability to forgive if they had not been so.

Jesus makes it unequivocally clear in Matthew 18 that <u>forgiveness</u> is central to the Gospel and must be central to our Christian lives.

You will remember the familiar passage. It starts in verse 21 with Peter asking the Lord how many times we must forgive each other. The answer (seventy times seven) really means that we must <u>always</u> forgive. There cannot be a limit. Forgiveness is central, Jesus says, to the Kingdom of God. If we cannot forgive those around us when they have wronged us, we either do not understand God's forgiveness to us —<u>all</u> of us — for the sins which we regularly commit in thought, word and deed — or we *reject it. If we cannot forgive people who wrong us, we are unaware of how much and how constantly we wrong God who, if we truly repent, will forgive us again and again. God's love is primarily expressed in forgiveness. That is the meaning of the Cross. If we don't forgive, we don't understand how much <u>we</u> need to <u>be forgiven</u> and we forfeit salvation. In this world, bitterness, obsession and isolation will take the place of love, fulfilment and contentment.*

Many Muslims in Iraq and Afghanistan, and no doubt elsewhere, will have strong reason to try to find forgiveness for Western military action, some of which has tragically killed innocent people. And who can blame them when they find this impossible? I expect that others here will have heard the chilling tape of one of the would-be aeroplane bombers in the recent trial. It was played on the radio news on Monday. This young Muslim's hatred was so intense, his desire for revenge so implacable, his declaration to teach us all a lesson so clear in its unitary horror, his belief in heavenly reward so pathetically misguided, that, let alone <u>forgive,</u> this young man and his associates were willing to kill thousands of innocent passengers on several aircraft as a response to offences, perceived or real, committed by others.

How this personification of destructive bitterness, unleashed in anger, contrasts with the words of Jesus on the Cross: 'Father, forgive them; they know not what they do.'

If we cannot forgive some-one, we cannot enter the Kingdom of Heaven because, in failing to forgive, we are failing to acknowledge our debt to God in His willingness to forgive us. We are all in this. Each one of us has failed in forgiveness at some point.

As I conclude in prayer, might I invite you, my brothers and sisters in Christ, to think of some-one whom you currently have not forgiven and then to join me, if you can, in this prayer?

'Lord Jesus Christ, I acknowledge that my salvation depends absolutely upon your forgiveness of my sins. I bring to you now a person (whom I name) whom I find it very hard to forgive. Now, at this moment, through the loving power of your Holy Spirit, release the bitterness I feel and help me to proclaim to you that I forgive this person, grateful in the knowledge that you have forgiven me. '

'Amen,' murmured the congregation.

ELEVEN

SITTING BETWEEN NORMAN AND JANE, the powerful words of Christian compassion challenged Mara. Their compelling, axiomatic goodness left no room for escape. Even if the whole thing were to be exposed as a fiction historically, its moral truth and ethical imperative were unanswerable. Forgiveness was the right thing to do. She could never put the horror behind her but the wound would gradually heal if she accepted this precept. She could try to live a positive life, helping others, perhaps: a Christian sort of life, even if the actual foundations of her belief were uncertain. Here were all these good people thinking good, positive thoughts. There was Christ on the Cross, forgiving those who were painfully murdering Him. Now, she was standing between Jane and Norman, not singing herself but taking in the words of the final hymn:-

'Love divine, all loves excelling.......'

Mara felt utterly disorientated. What was right? There could be no denying the dignity and beauty of what had been said, and was now being sung, even if she still had to be convinced about all the magic bits: the miracles and the Resurrection. But she had gone through fifty years without believing and this God of Love, whom these people were all worshipping, had stood back and allowed her husband to die from cancer and her daughter, with all her life ahead of her, to be brutally and horribly killed in a raging river. Surely the supernatural should have been controlling the merely natural. No, she couldn't take it- at least not yet. It is a fine story but it is unrealistic. She was still grieving with her terrible loss and, yes, she was terribly angry. Why didn't this God whom these people all revere step in at some point? Why did he allow Katie to meet that boy? Why did He contrive the horrible coincidence of the meeting on the tow-path after heavy rain? Why did that boy survive and not her daughter? No, no, no! She couldn't just jump ships like this. She found herself gasping for air. The din of the congregation as they sang the third verse now seared through her head:-

'Thee we would be always blessing,
Serve Thee as Thy hosts above,
Pray and praise Thee without ceasing,
Glory in thy perfect love.'

It was all wrong, wrong, wrong! She had to get out of this place.

Mara felt that she would burst. She could not respond to the soothing enquiries of Jane as they filed slowly up the congested aisle. Attempts at conversation had to compete with the hubbub around and the renewed music from the front. As they entered the crowded foyer, and her hosts were exchanging greetings with another couple, she made a dash for the door. She thrust her hymn book into the hands of a nonplussed Jean, dodged the outstretched hand of the visiting preacher and found herself at last in the cool, damp darkness of the street outside. She ran all the way to the next bus-stop, where she paused, trembling and alone.

A slow and confused journey back through the gloomy shadows and alien lights of the city concluded in a late number 45 depositing her near her home. Predictably, there were several messages on her voicemail from Jane expressing a crescendo of anxiety. She wearily deleted them all, took two sleeping pills with a glass of water and collapsed into bed.

She was woken at seven the next morning by another call from Jane. Groggy with the combined effect of the Flurazepam and the strain of the previous evening, and now finding herself so suddenly on the defensive, she had difficulty in achieving any sort of coherence and, absorbed in the disorientating wilderness of her own tragedy, she was wholly unable to connect with the predictably reasonable reaction of mystified incomprehension now being expressed by her sister-in-law.

'Mara, Dear, what's the matter? You must try to let us help you? You know that we are really concerned. Whatever went wrong last night? Norman and I have been worried sick all night.'

'I….I'm sorry. I don't know what came over me.'

'Would you like me to come over and see you now?'

'No, Jane, I couldn't put you to that trouble.'

'It would be no trouble, my Dear, you're understandably upset. I can catch a tram down this morning.'

Cornered, still partially anaesthetised in troubled sleep and unable to find a measured response to the insistent logic of this kindness, Mara lashed out.

'It's no use, Jane. That church service —it really got to me. How dare that man talk about forgiveness? He knows nothing about what it means. And all those people singing that rubbish about a loving God when I've lost Harry and Kate the ways I have. I don't want your religion and I'm just sick of you pestering me like this and trying to force it down my throat. Now just leave me alone! Don't phone me any more.'

She slammed the phone down and burst into tears. It had not crossed her mind that Norman and Jane knew nothing about Rob's admission.

As the season of Advent brought its message of bright hope into the darkening northern winter, encouraging social celebration even in a secular age, Mara rigorously imposed self-isolation. She could survive frugally on Harry's limited pension and life insurance. She shopped perfunctorily, preferring the bland anonymity of the supermarket to the threatening friendliness of local shopkeepers. She visited the cemetery regularly, keeping the grave of her loved ones tidy with fresh flowers through the grey December afternoons. As the early twilight descended and the Christmas lights decorated the busy evening rush hour, she would return to the empty house. She could not bear the television or radio; she never touched the computer. She could not concentrate even on reading, except for her favourite poem which she could now recite silently by heart:-

'I was angry with my foe;
I told it not, my wrath did grow.'

Her meals comprised baked beans or cheese on toast, or a boiled egg, or, occasionally, a pre-packaged fish pie, run through the microwave, washed down by a cup of tea made from a used tea-bag. Her natural bourgeois frugality prevented her from taking to drink but she did occasionally subdue the spectres which inhabited her insomnia with a sleeping pill. She did not bother to go out and clear the brown leaves from the garden. She gave up the ceremony of bringing the geraniums in for the winter. They would wither and die in their pots, victims of the first frosts. The roses, so cared for by Harry year by year, stood mournfully, unrelieved of their deadheads. The apple tree dropped its bright fruit, not garnered, food for birds and maggots. She became slovenly about dusting and tidying in the house. As she sat for hour after hour, looking into the darkness, even the sharp images of revenge began to fade. Her visual impression of Rob became less exact. Still, somehow, albeit now more vaguely defined, there was only one mission, one purpose in an otherwise meaningless life:-

'In the morning glad I see
My foe outstretched beneath the tree.'

Twice a week, she boarded the number 45 to Didsbury and walked down to the Mersey and along the river bank. Her single extravagance was the purchase of chrysanthemums. Each week she replaced them. She started by leaving a pink bunch on the bank at the fatal spot and throwing white flowers into the river one by one. Sometimes she varied the colours of the blooms on the bank: russet, yellow, mauve, deep crimson, but she always purchased white flowers to throw upon the water, pure white flowers, pure, like her darling dead daughter.

One afternoon, just as Mara was putting on her coat to walk to the bus, she was startled by the front door bell. It was her next-door neighbours, Cyril and Valerie Banks. She knew that, of course, she should invite them in but decided not to do so.

'We don't seem to have seen you for ages, Mara,' began Mrs Banks, standing awkwardly with her husband in front of the doorstep. 'We've been a bit concerned. Are you all-right?'

Mrs Banks was a retired primary school teacher, a sensible bespectacled woman with neatly permed grey hair and no-nonsense glasses.

Mara stiffened. 'It's very kind of you to call. Everything's fine, thank you.'

There was a strained silence. Mr Banks swivelled round slightly. Taking in the dead roses in the tiny front garden, which he must have observed dozens of times already, he clutched at an idea for a conversational gambit and offered to pop round to deal with them.

'That's very kind of you, Cyril but —no —I really ought to pull myself together and sort it out myself; it'll do me good.' She gave an unconvincing smile.

Mrs Banks certainly looked far from convinced. There was another awkward pause as Mara's visitors were kept standing in the chill dampness.

'Look, we don't want to interfere, Mara, but we know that things have been difficult for you…..' She faltered as her kind words seemed to enter a vacuum.

Her husband began to conclude the aborted communication.

'Just do let us know if you need anything —anything at all, now, won't you, Mara.'

'Even if it's just a little bit of company. You're always welcome to come round. Even if it's just a cup of tea,' said Mrs Banks.

'Or if you need a lift anywhere, it's no trouble to get the car out,' finished her husband.

'Yes, I'll bear that in mind. Thank you. It's been very good of you to call.'

They had no choice but to retreat and Mara shut the front door as soon as a minimal lapse for politeness permitted.

Mara and Harry had been very much a 'keep-themselves-to-themselves' couple, in the true, semi-detached, suburban English way. Pleasantries would be passed if neighbours chanced to meet on the pavement but it was not the convention much to enter each other's houses. Both the Banks and Miss Schofield, who was Mara's neighbour on the other side, had been there when the young Harry and Mara had first moved in a quarter of a century ago.

Elaine Schofield, too, a spry, if reclusive, eighty year old, had fulfilled social obligation by attending the funerals of both Harry and Kate. She would never have presumed to come to the door but she did pause when she met Mara on the street to enquire after her and to offer any help that might be appropriate.

There was no need for Mara to endure Christmas on her own. Despite the snub with which their kindness had been rewarded, Norman and Jane made two attempts to persuade her to go to them and Jane even made a point of saying that there would be no compulsory church. Valerie Banks called too, offering to include her neighbour at Christmas dinner when their daughter, son-in-law and grandchildren would be with them.

'It's very kind of you, Valerie, but I couldn't intrude like that.'

'It would be no intrusion at all, Mara - so long as you could cope with two lively children getting a little excited!'

'No, I just don't know if I'd cope —and I couldn't bear any sort of scene. It wouldn't be fair on other people —and you have your family. It's going to be a tough day but I'd rather cope with the grief on my own. I hope that you understand.'

It was indeed a tough day. She did in fact make a slight effort. She cleaned and tidied the house and bought a chicken to roast; she could enjoy the rest of it cold. She made sage and onion stuffing from a packet and roasted two potatoes. She opened a new bottle of cream sherry.

But it was no use. Rob's place of hatred in her imagination was replaced on Christmas Day by a desperate nostalgic longing for her husband and her daughter.

'I'm only fifty,' she wailed aloud. 'I deserve to have both of them in their prime.'

She put on a CD with carols from King's College, Cambridge, but cried so much that she had to turn it off. The seasonal music on Classic FM was interrupted by a banal presenter introducing a succession of happy families who had all met up for the day.

She looked at all the photographs of her beloved. At moments, she felt that they were both with her in the house. She conducted imaginary conversations with them aloud. But chill reality always won and she collapsed onto a chair in absolute desolation.

She was sleeping so badly, with chimeras of horror stalking the darkness, that, a few days into the New Year, she visited the doctor to request a prescription for some more sleeping pills.

'Of course, Mrs Braithwaite. Flurazepam again? And shall we stick with the stronger 30mg. version? It's not as though you are the kind of patient who is likely to misuse them,' smiled Dr Barrington. He was aware of her situation and felt sorry for her.

The surgery was near the bus-stop. She called into the supermarket for the flowers and caught the 45 towards the city. She realised that term had started again when some students boarded the bus at Parrs Wood. In recent days her mind had been more focused on Harry and Kate but, when a good-looking, smiling, dark–haired young man passed her inside the bus, she suddenly thought again about Rob. The revulsion welled up inside her like nausea. She alighted at Didsbury Village and walked through towards Northenden where she reached the footpath by the river. She came to the fatal spot. Just before Christmas, she had left some sprigs of holly in the usual place on the bank. It had seemed right to make that little alteration. Kate and Harry had both loved Christmas and she had lived for their happiness. Now, nearly three weeks later, the birds had eaten the berries and the leaves looked sad. She threw them into the swiftly flowing but opaque water. She had decided to buy two white bunches of chrysanthemums for the New Year. She propped one against a conveniently rigid osier. Then, one by one, she threw the flowers from the second bunch into the flood.

This, together with the visits to the cemetery, provided the ritual to her life.

'Oh, my darling, Katie. I love you so much and I miss you so dreadfully,' she said quietly aloud as the river snatched the frail blossoms. And then, as she threw the last one, 'Robert Hadfield, I will be revenged upon you for killing my lovely daughter. It may be the last thing I do but I shall do it.'

She had not stood outside the flat in Didsbury for some weeks and, as there was a thinner veil of cloud than usual, affording limited concession to a little weak wintry sunshine, she walked through to stand there for some time before the light started to fade. She waited and waited but, as on previous occasions when she had done this, there was no sign either of him or of the other students in the house. She just wanted to see him, to try to remind herself exactly of his appearance, to feed more precisely her revenge.

She caught the bus home before the congestion of the early rush hour. As she took her coat off, she found the Flurazepam in a pocket. She was about to put the small package away in the bathroom cabinet and then, suddenly, her torpor evaporated as she became animated with an idea. She smiled for the first time for ages. Suddenly, she looked, and felt, a little younger again.

TWELVE

Rob and Amélie were perched on stools, on either side of a high small round table, drinking Cappuccinos in a café tucked away in one of the narrow lanes between the Sorbonne and the Church of St Etienne du Mont. The windows steamed, obscuring the chill drizzle outside. Inside, however, it was warm, with the buzz of students arriving, meeting, greeting, leaving. At this time of the year, brightly coloured knotted woollen scarves and short navy or black coats, with collars turned up, were worn above blue jeans and trainers. Conversation was earnest, competitive, humorous.

'*Tu bois trop vite!*' complained Amélie as Rob drained his cappuccino in two gulps, wiping the foam from his upper lip.

'*Les fillettes font tout toujours lentement!.*'

'Oh! *Tais-toi!. Tu fais le bête!*'

Rob grinned as she pursed her lips and moved her shoulders with the merest hint of a Gallic shrug.

Rob and Amélie could both speak each other's language with considerable fluency. They moved between English and French with unplanned spontaneity. They had met the previous summer in Cahors. They had become Facebook 'friends' and were both pleased enough to discover that Amélie would be in her second year at the Sorbonne when Rob was taking his term out of Manchester to study there too. They had met quite a few times and had come to know -and like- each other quite well. Rob had benefited from a welcome into Amélie's social circle.

The monochromatic winter dampness extended northwards, shrouding the soaring Gothic splendour of Beauvais, the flat plains of Picardy, the cliffs of Dover, the parks of London. It confirmed the Midlands as sodden and unkind and intensified its special grip over Manchester, as of a being glad to be home again.

Although Jess still nominally lived in the Didsbury flat, she spent many nights with Eddie in Fallowfield. An old school friend was using Rob's room in his absence. Woody was thus the only member of the original quartet who was living there regularly. A calm chaos seeped across the establishment. Occasional mail arrived for Rob. Once, or even twice, Woody had rescued it from the floor and piled it randomly on a nearby shelf, prompted to do so after having trodden on it. Thus, Mara's carefully worded letter to Rob had received an imprint from the sole of Woody's trainers across its neatly written envelope, before finding itself lost between an unopened bank statement and an old school alumni circular sealed inside a transparent A4 polythene cover. Various items of junk mail had subsequently buried it deeper.

For a few days now, Mara had felt herself positively reviving. The gestation of a necessary plan and the act of commitment as it was set in motion had energised her.

Mr and Mrs Banks were invited in for a glass of Bristol Cream. They expressed genuine pleasure at seeing her 'beginning to pull through' like this. She busied herself tidying the house before they came. Dear me, she thought, how could I have let things get like this? The roses were at last dead-headed and the leaves swept up and incarcerated in black bags.

So it all went for a week or so. She took an interest in the daily arrival of the post. Every time a cold call came through on the phone she wondered if it might be Rob. Surely he would feel that he had to reply to her letter. And then, one day, when wondering about this, she suddenly remembered the computer. Of course! Young people only communicate electronically these days. She had never mastered texting on her mobile; surely Rob would remember that; Kate had joked about her mother being 'a dinosaur' more than once in his presence. But, although there were a number of unattended e-mails waiting, there was nothing from Rob. She went to her desk. The letter had been hand-written and she had written out a copy.

'Dear Rob,
I want to say how sorry I am for my appalling over-reaction. Please forgive me and put it down to shock and distress. Upon reflection, I realise, of course, that it was a horrible accident and that you had no intention to harm my darling Kate. I know very well that you loved her too and that you also feel her loss acutely. If there is anything for me to forgive, I do so now, freely.

Rob, I am sure that you will understand when I say that I find all this difficult to write. I am wondering therefore —indeed, I am asking —if you would come to see me, after all. It would clear the air for us both. I am pretty well free most of the time these days so, if you are willing to do this and I very much hope that you might be — just call me and we can fix a time. Perhaps you might care to come for tea?

Do please be in touch soon. I really look forward to hearing from you.

With sincere good wishes,
Mara Braithwaite.

The plan was simple really. She would add more sugar than usual to Rob's tea and add two or three crushed Flurazepam tablets to each cup. He would certainly drink at least two cups and so, at the very least, he would have consumed six double strength sleeping pills. Rob was unused to these and so he would react fairly quickly. When he fell into a deep sleep, she would kill him. She might use a kitchen knife; she might strangle him with one of Harry's ties. Mulling over the possibilities will provide a pleasantly interesting diversion. She would then take all the remaining sleeping pills herself and never wake up. There was no need to do so with mission accomplished.

However, several more days passed and there was still no communication from Rob.

Mara's mood began to darken once again. It looked as though Rob was ignoring her letter which might now be in a bin somewhere. She decided to take the 45 up to Didsbury. She would confront him; she would ask him if he had received the letter. Surely he could not then refuse her.

The next day, late in the afternoon, she took the bus towards the city centre. She alighted at Didsbury and walked to the house. No-one came or left. She actually rang the front door bell but there was no response. She tried again the following day, with the same result. On the third evening, she decided to wait as long as it took. It had been snowing a little the previous night and again in the morning. Now, in the darkness, the temperature sank to below freezing. Her spirits descended symbiotically. Was she to be deprived of any chance of revenge? Perhaps he had moved and was living somewhere else.

She was about to give her weary vigil up for the day when Woody came shambling up the road. Mara recognised him. As he fumbled with his keys, she crossed the road and greeted him. At first Woody did not know who she was. When she identified herself, she found it difficult to judge his response. She explained that she had written an important letter to Rob and wondered if he had received it. She guessed that Rob might have told Woody about the terrible scene and so judged it wise to mention that she had been very upset with Woody's friend and wanted to make amends. Woody genuinely did not know what she was talking about with regard to the letter.

'There are a few bits of mail here, Mrs Braithwaite, but I suppose they are going to wait till he gets back?'

'Ah, is he away? Will he be away long? Perhaps he is visiting his father in London?'

'No —he's away for much longer than that. The French part of his course has taken him to Paris for a stint. He's studying at the Sorbonne.'

Mara disguised her dismay and asked how long he might be there.

'I'm not quite sure. I think it's for the rest of the academic year….'

'Which means he won't be back until….?'

'October, I suppose. Another guy is renting Rob's room while he's away.'

Woody was not being artful or deceptive in saying this. He was naturally vague about matters to do with time and place and he had not really considered the exact duration of Rob's absence. He knew enough about this woman to dislike her but that had not influenced the inaccurate information which he had accidentally given. He did not even think about inviting her in to check through the mail.

They stood for a moment in the blackness of the January night into which Mara shortly dissolved. The pavement was icy and treacherous as she made her way to the bus stop. She had to wait longer than usual for the 45 and it was crowded when it eventually arrived. She suddenly felt terribly and purposelessly alone. All the passengers on the bus would have had homes to go to: families, friends. Her family had been taken from her and now the pernicious instrument of part of that cruel deprivation was beyond her reach. She dismissed the thought of getting a forwarding address in Paris from Woody. He would probably suspect her motives and she could hardly carry through any action of justice there anyway. Rob would obviously find it incredible that she should turn up in Paris to offer reconciliation. In any case, she had never been to France and the thought of attempting to travel there in January with a doomed mission was ridiculous. Some time ago, she had obliterated Rob's mobile phone number from both her address book and Kate's. In any case, she could not face the idea of speaking to him on the phone.

Back in Cheadle Hulme, Mara sat in the unheated darkness of the front room, allowing the welcome numbing of encroaching hypothermia to deaden her misery. A deep and mournful lassitude set in. The torpor was so all enveloping that she could not even find the will to get up and retire to the warm comfort of bed. As the days passed, she could no longer generate the animated fever of hatred or call forth specific images to excite the activity of revenge. She lost interest again in the housework and took care to avoid chance meetings with Mr and Mrs Banks or Miss Schofield. On the very few occasions when the phone rang, she did not answer it, fearing that it might be her sister-in-law, Jane.

Meanwhile, Woody had inadvertently destroyed his mobile phone. It had been a new one, replacing one which he had left on a bus a few weeks earlier. The circumstance seemed unjust because he had actually put half his clothes in the washing machine. Unfortunately the mobile had been in the pocket of his jeans. He had been sending texts to Rob fairly regularly and receiving replies. Now, he went on to Facebook. Three messages from Rob were awaiting his attention. They increased in sarcasm as the absence of any reply persisted. Woody decided not to respond on Rob's 'wall'; instead, he hit the 'message' button.

'Sorry, mate. I put my phone in the washing machine: bloody annoying as I'd only just replaced it. Glad you're having a good time in Paris — sounds pretty cool. All OK here apart from the weather. Usual Manchester shit. Watched United thrash Arsenal last Saturday. Ronaldo scored 2nd half. Eddie in a sulk —blames the ref.!! Bits & pieces of junk mail stacking up here —you don't want them sent on, do you? Seems odd not to be seeing you till next October —unless, that is, I get the Eurostar - which, come to think of it, I s'pose I could do at Easter — unless you're off with the lovely Emily (?) down to her place?'

Rob's reply came the next day.

'God — you are a Muppet! And — look —— I'm BACK at EASTER! I'm only here for a term. You knew that!! I told you! Dom's only got my room till then — unless, that is, he gets carted off to the nuthouse in the mean time, having to live with you!! Don't bother about the mail. None of it will matter. And she's called AMELIE,

not Emily- it's French, you know. Not surprising, since she is French!! Yeah, I saw part of the match on T.V. here. I loved the expression on Wenger's face when Ronny scored! Dig Eddie in the ribs for me! Seriously though, mate, I miss you. Be back all too soon. LOL.'

THIRTEEN

EASTER WAS LATE THAT YEAR. Spring had come to Paris with showery uncertainty while teasing with the coquettish promise of isolated bright sunny days.

One such was a Saturday in early April when Rob and Amélie took the train out to Versailles. Together, they had packed a picnic, buying fresh bread from a *boulangerie* in Versailles itself. They were disappointed to discover that, with its being the first decent Saturday of the year, it seemed that half the world had had the same idea. Rob asked an American emerging from the palace how long he had queued. It had been one hour and forty minutes, he said, and the queue, he added, smiling ruefully, was longer now than it had been when he was waiting.

They were about to give up the idea of the palace and simply enjoy the picnic in the palace garden instead when a young, uniformed, female attendant passed them.

'*Mademoiselle*' began Rob, '*Excusez-moi s'il vous plaît. Je me demande si peut-être il serait possible de nous asseoir. Je suis un étudiant anglais et malheureusement bientôt je devrais retourner en Angleterre. Aujourd'hui, nous manquons du temps pour faire la queue.*'

Rob paused, allowing the implication to float between himself and the young woman. He gave her his most persuasively engaging smile.

'*Vous êtes anglais?*' she replied, returning the smile and taking in both of them.

Before Amélie could utter a word, Rob had answered in the affirmative for them both. Amélie felt that she had no option other than to smile, keep quiet and nod rather foolishly.

The official paused while she considered the request. Rob added a slightly imploring touch to his second smile and apologised for making mistakes when speaking French.

After complimenting Rob '*pour son merveilleux français*', the young woman explained that she should not really do this but that there were tickets for admission available to members of the Versailles staff at a reduced cost and that her friend, Sylvie, held these at the *tabac* across the square. Rob immediately agreed not to tell anybody else in the ever extending queue. He was instructed to tell the said Sylvie that they were friends of Monique. Monique then produced her mobile and called Sylvie. Rob and Amélie offered words of profuse gratitude, stepped across the square and, sure enough, were expected by Sylvie who, upon confirming that they were Monique's friends, sold them the tickets at a greatly reduced tariff. They walked to the front of the queue and were inside the palace five minutes later. Amélie struggled not to have a fit of the giggles.

Soon, they were filing through the magnificence of the great state chambers, inhabited by the *Roi du Soleil* himself and his successors, culminating in the expulsion and execution of his great-grandson, Louis XVI and his queen, Marie-Antoinette. They saw the Le Brun ceiling in the King's State Apartment, with the planets gravitating around Apollo, the Sun God. They marvelled at the *Salle des Glaces* , gleaming and shimmering in all its splendour, with its chandeliers, its mirrors, its prospect over the formal gardens and Le Brun's paintings on the vaulted ceiling, illustrating the life of his great patron. They saw the bedchamber where Louis XIV died in 1715, after a reign of seventy-two years.

By now they were ravenous and it was time for the well supplied picnic to be transformed from a burden in their backpacks into a source of culinary pleasure. As if joining all else in acknowledging *Le Roi du Soleil* as its grand patron, the sun emerged with greater strength, brightly illuminating the long tree-lined avenues of the palace gardens with their precisely diminishing perspectives. On this particular Saturday, the fountains were playing in the formal garden. As if in harmony, an ensemble of musicians, dressed in the opulent elegance demanded by the court of the day, sat on the Parterre de l'Eau in front of the palace and played the Sun King's music: Lully, Couperin, Charpentier, Rameau: *la Gloire Baroque de la France, pendant le grand siècle d'Ancien Régime.* The gracious, balanced, civilised optimism of the music was relayed by discreetly placed amplifiers to the citizens strolling in the avenues or, as with Rob and Amélie, sitting to enjoy their picnic. The two young people ate pâté, Camembert, Pont l'Eveque, Boursin, salad and fresh baguettes, washing it all down with a crisp *Sèvre-Maine sur lie*, which Rob had kept in a portable cooler. They were fortunate to find a vacant bench on the parterre, with an uninterrupted view of the great Fontaine de Latone and the front of the palace.

In due course, they took the train back and, as had become their custom of late, kissed formally as they parted company at Champs de Mars station. Rob sat for a while, looking across the Seine. He heard the muffled commentaries in the *Bateaux Mouches* as they glided past on the calm water, the tourists on board pointing their cameras towards the Eiffel Tower behind him.

Families walked past, overtaken by younger joggers wearing t-shirts and shorts. As he sat by this path by this different river, the familiar dark thought was triggered in his mind; it was never far away. Yet again he rehearsed the dreadful moment when Kate had slipped into the raging Mersey. Yet again, he wondered just how responsible he was for the accident. Yet again, the expression of pure, furious hatred which disfigured Mara Braithwaite's face, when he had last seen her, haunted him, coming between him and the springtime happiness of the Parisian scene around him.

Then, his reverie drifted further back. Out of the darkness appeared the torn, tear-stained visage of Lydia: Lydia, who had tried so hard to comfort him after his mother had died: Lydia, whom he had met, shimmering and ethereal, at a school dance when they were both in the Lower Sixth at neighbouring schools: Lydia, who had given him his first taste of erotic love: Lydia, with whom he had secretly slept after the Leavers' Ball at school: Lydia, whose apparently limitless fund of compassion had in the end driven him mad during the days of unimaginable horror following his mother's funeral: Lydia, whose very comfort became an oppression so overwhelming that he had ended it with abrupt simplicity by slapping her once across the face: Lydia, who, since, through no fault of her own, had added guilt to his misery.

He willed the fearful apparitions away, forcing himself to think of Amélie instead. He liked Amélie very much. She was much more fun and less clinging than Kate. Her *joie d'esprit,* her animated friends of both sexes (who had so quickly and unreservedly included him as a *Mitglied* to their companionable circle), her total lack of prissiness and fuss, all recommended themselves to him. She was pretty too, with her quick dark eyes and her lips pouting with pretended disapproval at every surprise or challenge. More widely, there was something satisfyingly exotic about his assuming the part of a French student, not least because it was a role verifiably discrete from the recent horrors of his life in Manchester: a different world, inhabited by different people who spoke a different language. He wondered again about Amélie. No, there was nothing more to it than a very good friendship. And that suited him very nicely, as, he suspected, it did Amélie. Indeed, this particular set of friends at the Sorbonne seemed to survive very happily without the fragile tensions, jealousies and exclusions which afflicted couples hiving off into premature partnerships. There was a freedom and openness which he welcomed. This pattern of thought brought him to consider Woody; yes, Rob thought, Woody, with his self-contained, accepting autonomy, would fit into this scene well. It was a pity that it would all come to an end in a fortnight's time. He realised how little he was looking forward to the return to Manchester or, indeed, to the gloomy care dispensed by his father in London. Still, he would enjoy what was left of this happy experience in Paris. Rob treated himself to an ice-cream being sold from a temporary stall nearby and, as he sat and licked it, he admired two slender, pretty girls walking past, wearing four inch heels and very short skirts.

FOURTEEN

A FORTNIGHT LATER, AFTER HAVING spent a lugubrious week-end with his father, Rob was back in Manchester, smacking hands with Eddie and giving Woody a manly hug.

Meanwhile, had Mara Braithwaite ever read 'The Waste Land', she might possibly have agreed that 'April is the cruellest month.' The snowdrops in February had given her no joy. She had greeted the bright daffodils, as they braved a blustery March, with loathing. And now the tulips, bulbs planted by Harry, taunted her with a life and hope for ever lost. The blackbirds, once her friends and welcome visitors, now irritated her as they proclaimed the joys of courtship and procreation in their loud and liquid song. Soon, hateful Easter would be upon her, celebrating its tidings of false hope with blossom of pure white. It seemed right that vicious squally showers should thrash and scatter the pathetic petals to the ground.

This particular morning, Mara did not even bother to dodge the showers that had bedevilled the city for the last two weeks. She let a hail-storm sting her face and drench her clothes as she made her way to the off licence and the florist. Suddenly, she could not bear the social meeting point of the supermarket; in any case, it was further away.

When she returned to the house, she set about destroying letters and photographs. She pitched once treasured wedding presents, together with ornaments formerly of sentimental value, into black bags.

'Having a good clear-out?' the young dustman had enquired, cheerfully enough.

'My Nan's been doing the same. I guess that, when you get older, stuff begins to pile up and it's time to do a bit of spring cleaning.'

Mara nodded and brought the wheelie-bin back for a refill.

Tired with her effort, and too preoccupied with her misery to remember to cook a meal or turn the heating on, she once again sat motionlessly in the chair in front of the unlit gas fire. As the day darkened into evening, another hail-storm clattered against the house in sharp bursts of fury. She did not think about switching a light on or drawing the curtains, once so carefully chosen from John Lewis. Somewhere outside a gate banged repetitively. A distant car alarm bleeped hopelessly. Intermittently, jets passed overhead with a muffled roar as they descended to Ringway Airport. As night came on, the weather stilled and all was enveloped in blackness, save for the limited beams from a street-light further along the road. She sat there all night, finally succumbing to a fitful doze for a couple of hours or so.

The imaginative enterprise and physical effort involved in carrying through her plan to do away with Rob had for some time been dulled by weariness and ennui. Her dangerously all-consuming introspection notwithstanding, she had even managed to realise for herself the melodramatic absurdity of her different schemes. It would never work. The boy would already be recovering and living a full and vibrant life elsewhere. She was beyond caring. Indeed, the idea of seeing him again was abhorrent. How could she have ever imagined otherwise? He was in the past, like everything else in her life. Good and bad merged into colourless obscurity. There was no future.

When daylight came the next morning, Mara tidied the kitchen, locked the house and placed the Flurazepam tablets and the bottle of vodka, recently purchased, in a plastic bag, together with a bunch of white narcissi still in its cellophane wrapping. She put her raincoat on (a straightforward garment, bought at Marks and

Spencer's, but smart enough at the time) and caught the 45 up to Didsbury.

She left the bus at Fletcher Moss and walked down to the river. She soon came to the familiar fateful spot. One by one, she extracted the flowers and threw them into the water. Once again, after the punishing rain, the Mersey was flowing fast, heedlessly swirling westwards to the Irish Sea. Once again, Mara imagined her daughter falling into the maelstrom, then spun round helplessly like a child's doll and, finally, sucked underneath by the irresistible aquatic force. The delicate white flowers were engulfed into oblivion the moment they touched the water.

'Oh, my darling,' she murmured softly, 'if only I could believe I was coming to join you- but it's impossible and I can't carry on in this miserable world. And Harry, where were you when all this happened to our precious daughter? Oh, my love, I can't lie on that bed again without you —your warmth, your love, your sweet voice. We were true in love. That was something, but it's finished; there is nothing left; there is no hope.'

She opened the packet of Flurazepam, took three tablets from the foil which encased them and put them inside her mouth. Then she unscrewed the top of the bottle of vodka and took a large swig to wash the sleeping pills down. She had never drunk vodka before. The fiery, overpowering spirit stung the roof of her mouth, the fumes exhaling through her nose, but it dispatched the tablets as effectively as the river had washed away the flowers. Mara repeated this process several times until there were no tablets left. Her stomach retched; she felt sick; she fell backwards against the osier bush; her head was swimming. She embraced the accelerating descent into unconsciousness with relief.

∾

Rob had maintained his running in Paris. On some days, he would cross the Boulevard St Germain, traverse the river via Ile de la Cité, run eastwards along the *Quai* and return across the Pont de Sully. As an alternative, he sometimes ran to the Odéon, then turned into the Luxembourg Gardens and continued along the Avenue de L'Observatoire as far as Montparnasse. Although running for oneself is a solitary sport, Rob was far from alone on these early mornings. Young Parisians passed him in the opposite direction, the girls chic with their tightly fitting shorts clutching their thighs, their t-shirts moulded round their bras, their hair held back by bands, the slim young men wearing baggy shorts which reached to their knees, exposing pale shins above short socks and trainers. Some faces became familiar and there were smiling nods of acknowledgement, breath too precious to expend articulating greeting.

Determined not to compromise his fitness, Rob quickly recommenced his running when he returned to Manchester. The route seemed depressingly familiar. He strove hard to keep his mind clear but, of course, it was impossible to banish images of Kate. It was his first time along the terrible tow-path since his return. He took a deeper breath and increased his pace. He knew the dreadful spot all too well but this morning he was surprised to see a figure there. It was a woman and it seemed that she was sitting on the path, propped up in a somewhat unnatural posture by one of the osiers growing along the levée behind the tow-path. He instinctively realised that there was something wrong. He slowed down, preparing to investigate.

He gave a sharp intake of breath when he recognised Mara Braithwaite. She was in a bad way but was still just about conscious. Rob saw the nearly empty vodka bottle and an empty packet which had contained pills. She had been violently sick. He bent down and tried to raise her to an upright sitting position.

'Oh —Mrs Braithwaite- what have you done? Don't say that you've drunk all this vodka. What was in the packet? Oh, my God!'

Her mouth was open. Her eyes stared without recognition. The raincoat, always freshly dry cleaned, lay crushed beneath her, soiled by the dirt on the tow-path.

She retched again. He cradled her head in his arm and tried to get her to sit up. She showed no sign of recognition.

'It's me —Rob! What the Hell have you done? I'll call for an ambulance.'

This time he had his mobile with him. He dialled 999 and communicated the nature of the emergency.

She seemed to be collapsing in his arms and drifting further out of consciousness.

'Hey! Mrs Braithwaite! It's me, Rob! I've called the ambulance. They'll be here very soon.'

At this second mention of his name, Mara managed to turn her head slightly. She seemed to take in the identity of her self-appointed rescuer. She emitted a sort of deep growling gurgle and fixed her eyes on him.

Rob realised immediately that these were eyes of unforgiving hatred and, even amidst the intensity of this present emergency, he felt the shock of sudden fear produced by this extraordinary intimacy of concentrated enmity. He had never before encountered personal hatred and, for a moment, it distracted him from the practicalities of the immediate task. He tried to support her but she found a sort of strength which allowed her to struggle against his protection. Rob could not let her collapse prone onto the path; he held her more firmly. He realised that she was in a critical condition but he knew intuitively the only thing in her mind at that moment.

'The ambulance is coming, Mrs Braithwaite. I am going to try to save you. How could you have done such a terrible thing?'

She found three simple words at last and, struggling for concentration, breath and coordination of her tongue, rasped,

'I HATE YOU.'

'Don't say that!' Tears suddenly forced themselves through his eyes.

Again, yet more feebly but with no less menace, 'I HATE YOU.'

She still fixed her eyes on him, as though casting a spell.

'I am so, so sorry about what happened here. I didn't push Kate. Honestly, I didn't. I wouldn't have ever done such a terrible thing. I'm not like that. You've got to believe me! Please! Please!' He was aware that his voice was turning into a low wail. 'It WAS an accident —a terrible accident.'

She had given up struggling but she still glared at him with unblinking hostility.

'It was an accident —for which I was to blame. Oh, I'm so sorry. I'd do anything to turn the clock back, Mrs Braithwaite. PLEASE forgive me. You've got to forgive me! I NEED you to forgive me. PLEASE, Mrs Braithwaite! Mara!'

She could no longer muster the strength to find words. But, without losing the grip of her stare, she used her last mortal strength to shake her head ever so gently.

Still holding her in his arms, Rob released sobs of anguish as Mara Braithwaite breathed her last.

FIFTEEN

'My dear Son, what an ordeal you've had!'

Father and son were back in Oriel's. The waiter had received their order. Chelsea inhabitants were eating pasta around them, each table cocooned in its private world of conversation, rehearsing the day's conflicts, successes, amusements, frustrations, anxieties, ambitions. The waiter poured two glasses of *Montepulciano d'Abruzzo*. Brian Hadfield drank a mouthful of tap-water.

Rob was silent. For once, he could not make the running in the conversation.

The father watched his son with discreet compassion.

'Dad, I…I…..' He could not get started.

'Don't worry, Son. There's no need to say anything.'

For more than a minute neither of them did.

'Just so long as you know that I'm always here for you.' Then, with the most restrained of smiles, 'That won't ever change.'

'Thank you, Dad.'

Rob was genuinely grateful but could not manage to say any more.

Brian Hadfield thanked the waiter as a small plate of mixed olives and feta cheese was placed on the table.

'She just refused to believe me, Dad. She actually thinks —thought —that I deliberately pushed Kate into the river.'

He bent his head and covered his eyes with his hands. Apart from one conversation immediately after his mother's death, this was possibly the nearest approach to an intimate exchange with his father that Rob could remember having had.

'Well, it should go without saying that nobody else will have thought that. Any-one who knows you at all would realise the absurdity of such an accusation.'

'I know, Dad. But, in a way, I sort of DID. If we hadn't had that struggle, Kate would be alive now. So would Mrs Braithwaite.'

Brian Hadfield did not rush in. Of all men, he knew how facile words could be. Although his own intense suffering had involved the pain of bereavement, he did possess, behind the securely sustained façade of reserve, an emotional and imaginative depth which allowed him to understand something of the misery of guilt. He believed that his son should not feel guilty but he also believed that Rob possessed a strongly defined morality and he knew with sad concern that a few glib clichés, swiftly delivered, would contribute nothing of value.

'Although you won't be able to agree for some time yet, you are being too hard on yourself, Son. Just because that poor, bereft, demented woman could not find it in herself to forgive you, does not mean that you should not forgive yourself. And you have much less to forgive than she was accusing you of.'

Rob shook his head and looked wearily across the table at his father.

'Do talk about it if you think it would help,' his father added.

There was an interruption when the main course arrived. After the waiter had fussed around them with black pepper and grated parmesan, Brian Hadfield started to speak in a way which his son had never heard before.

'You know, Rob, when your Mother died, I just could not talk about it with any-one, including you, my only son. Like you, I have no brothers and sisters and my parents, your grandparents, had passed on. I did not think it right to burden you, a boy, still at school, with my outpourings of grief. In any case, I am such a stupidly private man that I could not begin to share my feelings with anyone at all. But you, Rob, are different from me. You inherited your mother's naturally outgoing personality. I loved that about her and I envy it in you —not in some unpleasant way, you understand, but in deep respect. The time has probably not come yet but I really hope that you will be able to share your feelings in a way which has always been impossible for me and to share your great hurt and confusion with another human being —perhaps with one of your close friends, or (and I speak as some-one who has not been attentive to church going) with a priest; they do have wisdom, experience and confidentiality. Or, I would be very willing to pay for a psychotherapist if you felt that that might help. And, of course, if you ever felt —and there is no obligation at all — that you wanted to share it with me, I would try hard to do my best by you. You have been through a double trauma, my dear boy —indeed a triple one when we include your dear mother.'

He paused briefly.

'But —I'm sorry, Son. I hadn't intended to say so much. Don't feel that you've got to respond - not at this moment, anyway. Come on, we'd better eat this before it gets cold. Look! We haven't even started to drink our wine yet!'

Rob was nonplussed. He had never received such confessional intimacy from his father before. Nor had he understood his father's capacity to support him.

'Oh Dad! My dear Dad!'

He could manage no more. Grabbing the table napkin, he got up and hurried to the lavatory.

Brian Hadfield started to rise and follow him but immediately realised that that would be a mistake. He sipped his glass of wine thoughtfully and carefully wound some strips of pasta round his fork.

~

Showery April that year surrendered to a smiling, sunny May. Manchester had shrugged off the stained brown and drab grey rags of a damp, gloomy autumn and a dark protracted winter. The pale garbs of a snivelling, reluctant spring were also suddenly discarded and replaced by bright greens and reds and blues and purples, all in different shades and hues, scented clean and fresh.

It was a Saturday and the patio door at Norman and Jane's house was open. Bustle and merriment filled the house and the garden as this couple, now in their late fifties, celebrated their Silver Wedding Anniversary. Childless themselves, they had invited many of their friends from the church round for a buffet. The gathering ranged from the new born baby belonging to the earnest young youth pastor and his pretty wife to a smiling incapacitated lady in her nineties, sitting contentedly on a firm garden chair. Inside, cards festooned the mantelpiece and brightly wrapped presents accumulated in the hall. Good will and happiness complemented the weather. The ladies had combined to bring a vast confection of quiches, cold meats, pâtés and salads. Jane had cooked an enormous salmon and assembled a vast and varied fruit salad. Norman was liberal in dispensing wine from his case of Argentine Chardonnay, though many of the church ladies were happier drinking the alternative elderflower cordial. Every-one was keen to help.

'You sit down, Jane. It's your special day. Stop all this working and go and chat to some of your visitors.'

'No, Love, I'm fine. I'm getting round to see people too.'

'That salmon looks a treat —with the asparagus heads round it and the grapes on top. I don't know how you had time to do all that. Aren't you clever?'

'Oh, it was nothing really, Sarah: just a bit of organisation yesterday. And Norman's really very good.'

A bright, bespectacled fifteen-year-old boy, who travelled south through the city every weekday to attend the Manchester Grammar School, was politely but assiduously tapping into Norman's knowledge of Victorian Manchester to help him as he put together an assignment on Free Trade. The lad's parents were much involved in supporting the church in a multitude of ways. His younger sister and a friend, meanwhile, were making eyes at good-looking young Ben, the father of the new baby, under whose management they all met at the youth group every Friday evening.

'Come on then, Norman, Love. Bill's glass is empty over there. William, you shouldn't encourage him! Sorry if I'm breaking up an intellectual conversation between you two!'

'All-right, Jane. William and I were just discussing Cobden and Bright. He's writing an assignment on them for school. He seems to know a lot about them! '

Jane bustled off to tidy up an ashet of cold ham. Jean, the retired spinster librarian, moved alongside her.

'What a lovely celebration, Jane: a very happy day for every-one —most of all, of course, for Norman and you. '

'Well, Jean. What makes it so special is to have all our friends around us. And God has been so good to us both. We keep well enough and we have such a wonderful church family. It's a real support.'

'You're the ones who support most of us.'

"No, no! We all support each other. That's what it's all about, isn't it? 'Love thy neighbour'. And our church certainly does its best to obey that. Look at all that <u>you</u> do: working out the sidesmen's rota, the flower rota, getting in the quarterly Bible reading notes from the Scripture Union. We'd be lost without you, Love!'

'Thank you Jane. Changing the subject, I haven't really had a chance to say how I sorry I was to hear about Harry's sister-in-law. What a dreadful thing! I suppose that the poor lady never got over losing her daughter so tragically.'

'No, I'm afraid she didn't. It was a very sad business —and a lot to ask <u>anybody</u> to cope with. She didn't share our faith, of course. She got very cross with us when we tried to suggest that that might be a way through the valley of the shadow. We so wanted to help Mara; she was so dreadfully unhappy. I'm afraid that she just turned in upon herself, feeling that everything —and everybody —was against her.

You know, Jean, bitterness is a terribly self-destructive emotion. It just eats you up. After all, you're a single lady, Jean, with no family (we've talked about this before, haven't we?). And, think of Norman and me! Everyone sees us as being so cheerful. It seems as though we haven't a care in the world. But yet —we'd have loved to have children. Just look at the way Norman was getting carried away with that lad from M.G.S.. Norman would love to have had a boy who might have shared his interests like that. But it wasn't to be- for us, or for you. And yet the Lord has blessed us in so many other ways —and perhaps it's left us free to help others in ways that might not otherwise have been possible.'

They were interrupted by a loud clapping of hands on the patio. The pastor, who was not much older than Ben, his youth worker, having swapped his winter jeans for a pair of long military camouflage shorts, was, at the invitation of Norman, summoning the assembled company. He congratulated the couple on their anniversary, briefly and appropriately spoke words of thanks for all they have contributed to the church fellowship over many years, and offered thanks to God for them and for the food which was being consumed.

Norman, in turn, thanked the pastor, beginning his short oration with the words, 'It falls to me…..'

Every-one then ate and talked and smiled and looked out for each other. Not a cloud was to be seen in the Manchester sky that day.

∼

The mild spring developed into a warm early summer. Rob and Amélie had walked along the Avenue Kleber and, having crossed the Place du Trocadero, were standing on the steps of the Palais de Chaillot, looking across the Seine to the Eiffel Tower. It was a clear evening and the prospect was dramatic, augmented by the purple blossom below them in the foreground, before the Pont d'Iena. The setting sun was casting a golden glow over the Champs de Mars and, in the intermediate distance, its radiance was reflected from the dome of Les Invalides.

'Earth hath not anything to shew more fair,' said Rob quietly.

'Quoi?' asked Amélie, looking up at him interrogatively.

'Wordsworth: a great English poet —only he was describing <u>London</u> and it was the <u>morning</u>.'

Rob broke into a chuckle and put his arm round her shoulder. Amélie put hers round his waist. He bent down and they kissed.

'Come on,' he said. "It's a lovely evening. Let's cross the river and walk back. I'm going to treat us to dinner at 'L'Etoile du Berger'. They do fantastic *escargots* and *'The Confit de Canard* must be the best around. The *patron* is a really nice guy too.'

'Eh bien! C'est cher n'est ce pas? Pourquoi çe soir?'

'C'est pour toi, ma petite! Pour nous! Vraiment pour nous! Et ….' He felt it could only be said in English. 'It is an anniversary: some-one I met a year ago today: a difficult anniversary, Amélie. The person —who was very important to me —is now dead. It was a girl-friend, back in England. Please don't ask me about it. Her death was horrible. But this is the day I'm putting it behind me. I'm laying the ghost to rest. Well…. I suppose that is easier said than done. The shadow is bound to darken the brightness from time to time but today —this evening —I'm resolved to stand against it for the first time: to look forward rather than backwards. Anyway……my father has just sent me some money, instructing me to spend it on something like this. So —let's go! What are we waiting for? I'm ravenous!'

ABOUT THE AUTHOR

PETER FARQUHAR WAS BORN IN Edinburgh and grew up in London. He graduated in English from the University of Cambridge. He has extensive experience in teaching, including having been the Senior English Master at the Manchester Grammar School, Head of English at Stowe and Lecturer at the University of Buckingham. His novel, *Between Boy and Man*, was published in 2010.

Ingram Content Group UK Ltd.
Milton Keynes UK
UKHW041340190723
425432UK00001B/27